I0622070

THE
GRIM
KEEPERS

An Anthology of Spooky Stories
Written by 15 International Authors

ISBN 13: 978-0692553398
ISBN 10: 0692553398

DEDICATION

This book is dedicated to all writers who aspire to be published. Make connections, reach out to other writers, and dare to dream. This book was written by 15 people who came together in an online writing community and threw around ideas that became an exciting, scary anthology. The team chose the name, the cover, and critiqued each other's work to give you the best reading experience possible. We have some very established writers and some newcomers. Keep writing, keep believing, and keep dreaming!

ABOUT CW PUBLISHING HOUSE

CWPH is a new publishing company, set up with the primary goal of publishing CWC Collaborative Fiction Novels. CWPH intends to open its doors to all forms of Collaborative Fiction in 2016, and has plans to publish a wide variety of Anthologies. For more information, please visit:

www.cwpublishinghouse.com

Summer is Dying...

Her energy is spent and waning. Collapsed on the forest floor, her body drifts steadily into decay. The cool autumn wind sings her eulogy through the veining limbs as trees lose their amber-honey leaves. The bride of our sultry season beckons us to meet her with corpse-like fingers. And in her horrid state she will not be denied. Her entreaties, hyphenated by malice for refusal, ask you to lay down on a mattress of moldering leaves to fall asleep beside her. She has macabre tales to whisper into you, and she insists that you listen!

By Roy Laurence Daman

The Grim Keepers

CONTENTS

Title: Author:

The Grim Keepers

And You Will Not Be Afraid
By Kathrin Hutson

The bus was cold. I pulled my jacket closer around my shoulders and tightened my grip on the handlebar overhead as the bus made a sharp, bumping turn. My other hand fingered the silver cross hanging from my neck—not out of faith so much as habit. I had all but completely lost the faith. My fingers kept the muscle memory.

The bus stopped to let me out. I hadn't asked for a stop, I didn't know where we were, but it was the last drop-off on the bus route before the driver had to turn around and start it all over again. So, why not get out now?

I headed down the few stairs toward the bus doors as they hissed open, thanked the driver, and stepped outside. A gust of wind hit me, and I turned my back to repel it, hearing only the revving of the bus as it left me in the road.

My eyes caught on a bright yellow piece of paper dancing across the street—a flier. The wind died down, and the paper landed face up in front of me. I read it from where I stood.

Saint Elizabeth's School
For Young Girls
Come to our Open house
Sunday, October 30th
1342 S. Preston St.

Below these words was a black and white print of a large estate house—big enough, grand enough, old enough to be a boarding school. Private and religious, no doubt.

As soon as I had swept my eye over the printed building, the wind built up again, tearing the flier from me. I whipped my head to look after it, but it was soon lost, flapping between the trees and climbing higher. *Oh well.*

I turned toward the side of the street and stopped. Frowning, I blinked several times, but it was still there. The house. St. Elizabeth's School for Young Girls—right in front of me. I glanced behind me quickly, sure that somebody would be laughing at my surprise. But the streets were empty except for the few last leaves falling off the near-bare trees. I sighed, the wind pushing me toward the building, and so I went to it.

Now that I saw this place in reality, I felt suddenly drawn to it. It was a large, white plantation house, three pillars in the front on the porch and two plank swings hanging on one of the large oak trees. I counted twenty small windows on the second floor, and the walls of the ground level floor were simply windows, separated by the front door and what I thought would be a hallway inside. The grass was green and well-groomed, even this late in the fall, and the large building seemed freshly painted and well-kept. Another gust of wind blew, and I heard a wind chime dangling on the front porch. The rest of the silence was almost too eerie.

As I stepped both feet onto the walkway that cut up the middle of the yard toward the porch, the great oak front door opened, and a jangle of conversing voices flooded out. The people followed.

Most of them were older women, those probably here as grandmothers or older mothers of those 'pretty little Catholic girls' they wanted to send to a respectable and unisex boarding school. They flooded out in their flower-print dresses and floppy sun hats. The sun had come out suddenly, as if just for them, and the wind died down. It was fall, yet it suddenly felt like mid-summer. I stopped, gazing at the porch as it steadily filled with chatty women.

One in particular, a significantly portly old woman with dimpled cheeks, droopy eyes, and a tightly drawn bun of gray hair caught sight of me, and immediately dismissed herself to head my way. I noticed all she wore was a loose, plain brown dress that hung away from her body as it passed her jutting chest. She waddled to me, and took my hand in hers. My arm went awkwardly slack in her grasp and I tried to be gentle. She did not look like she could break easily—she was weather-worn and year-tried—but I did not know her.

"Hello, deary, hello," she exclaimed, and patted my hand exuberantly, smiling from rosy cheek to rosy cheek. I returned a fake smile and a quick nod, glancing about uncomfortably. "You must be here for the open house."

"Umm, not really," I answered slowly. "Really, I just…" To tell the truth, I didn't even know why I *was* here. Telling her that I'd seen the flier wouldn't have convinced her of the coincidence.

The woman caught a drift of my discomfort and laughed heartily, her body bouncing. "Well, no matter. No matter at all. Come join us. After all, the operative word is *open*. Have some lemonade." Her grip tightened on one of my hands and she dragged me across the yard toward the other chittering women. "Oh, by the way," she began again. "My name is Bernadette, and I'm the dean of this school." She said this rather slowly, her voice bouncing through highs and lows. She asked me my name. I couldn't answer for the suddenly dry state of my mouth, but as soon as I opened it to say something, anything, she squealed in delight and handed me a Dixie cup of lemonade.

I took an unconscious sip, watching all these old women, not feeling particularly included —I had no idea what the school was like at all— but not feeling particularly left out, either. I was just here. I sat on one of the nearby plank swings, setting the cup down, and pushed my feet back and forth. I kept thinking it was such a nice day.

Another woman, one much younger than the others yet still older than myself, came to sit beside me on the other swing. She had flaming red hair and soft eyes that made her look rather tired. We introduced ourselves, she explaining that she had an older daughter she wanted to transfer here, and then she asked me why I wore such dark clothing for a day like this. I could not come up with an answer for the life of me. What did it matter?

"Black just makes you seem so…dreary," she began in a slow voice. And then she carried on about the negativity of black, such as my jacket. I sighed, preparing to never find someone interesting to talk to while I was here, and I glanced around the gigantic front yard of the school. My eyes stuck on the oak front door, glistening brown in the light, and then it opened.

My heart jumped to my throat and stopped beating there. An occupied woman let herself onto the porch from inside, but I did not pay attention to her. I could see perfectly down the hallway leading into the school, and it seemed to loom closer and grow more pressing the longer I stared at it. All the sound from the surrounding women faded away, and the extent of my awareness suddenly lay within that doorway. I had to get in there.

Distractedly, I excused myself from the red-head's company and made my way across the lawn to the front porch. My eyes never left the doorway and my heart never seemed to start working again. I felt pulled—pulled by some invisible line attached to the core of my being— and I even tried to pull away, just once, but to no avail. Slowly, I stepped both feet onto the oak floors, my hand brushing the matching door, and I was inside.

The ceiling loomed above me, seemingly ever upwards, and I gazed upon the vast white walls and the huge portraits of aged women that hung there. To my left, a large room filled with the light cascading through the windows, duplicated in the room to my right. I walked down the short hall, which emptied out into an even grander room. In the center sat a huge staircase, winding up to the second floor banisters that towered over my head. I took this all in for a moment longer, then walked on.

Moving further toward the back of the school, I came to another staircase, not as large as the first, but still as striking. The floor back here had changed to a white tile, and even my own sneakered feet clicked against them. A much greater number of women bustled about now, far unlike the others who had come to view the school; they worked here.

The Grim Keepers

Most were older as well, of all shapes, dressed in white, crisply pressed maid smocks. They reminded me more of nurses' uniforms, yet I doubted that's what they were. They clamored about with trays of food and pitchers, some with armloads of laundry. A few passed by with little girl's arms clasped in their hands, hastily taking them to and fro for some important this or that. I heard clanking and rushing water coming from further on, and guessed that must have been the kitchen. I turned another corner to find one more staircase, hidden from me behind wide, windowed double doors. I saw the stairs vaguely through the small square windows, and my curiosity grew intense enough to burst.

I headed toward those doors, then realized that everyone around me, the maids and the little girls, had stopped doing what they had just been so busy to do. Most of the maids gave me a wary eye and slowly continued to their destinations, wanting to watch but obviously unwilling to involve themselves. Some, however, merely stopped and stared. I caught sight of a lone girl who had just come from the kitchen, and she leaned against the wall that encased the following staircase. She did not seem shy, nor afraid of me as some of the women had. But I had the odd sensation she knew something that I didn't.

I took another step toward the staircase, watching the girl. Her eyes widened and she shook her head at me ever so slowly, almost in warning. Trying both to ignore her and to fight the invisible line that still drew me to the staircase, I stepped forward. I came within two feet of the small windows in the doors, and peering up to look in, the sight there froze my blood.

A girl sat on the staircase, her knees drawn up to her chin. Her face was completely invisible behind a cascade of greasy, wild dark hair, caked with all kinds of grit that I couldn't make out and hanging in strings down her face. The dress she wore turned my stomach. It was ripped, torn, and soiled beyond imagination. I could tell by the crumbs, drips of food, scattered feces, and the yellow stains on the front of her dress that no one had bothered to clean this girl. No one had bothered to help her at all. A mixture of pity and rage filled me and I tried to catch my breath. Had these people just left her in here?

I turned around swiftly and glared at one of the nearby maids. "What's wrong with this girl?" I demanded, looking wildly around. "Isn't it your job to take care of her?" The maid I accused simply stood there dumbfounded, and like the well-kept little girl leaning against the wall, simply shook her head. What was wrong with these people?

I turned to the double doors of the staircase again and thrust them open. The maid outside screamed, and suddenly the dirty girl on the staircase jerked her head up to look at me. Her eyes met mine, and I flung my hands over my face, wanting to wipe the picture out of my memory. I backed quickly out of the doors, leaving them to swing violently back and forth before me, and stared into the staircase again. The girl had lowered her face once more.

Disgusted and utterly horrified, I realized my fingers had gone numb. The girl's face had been the palest of whites, and I had seen every vein beneath her skin glowing blue with the most awful strain. Tear stains had streamed down that face, caked up against blotches of mud and crumbs, ruining the young face. And those eyes. The eyes that had glared back at me from under the matted hair were black. All pupil and no color —no soul with which to identify another human. They were evil eyes, those which dared me to touch her and cursed me for thinking of it. They were eyes that pleaded for help.

As quickly as doors had settled I heard

more screaming from behind me. I whirled around wildly only to encounter the second most horrible sight. A massive, snarling black dog came barreling around the corner, fangs bared and jowls overflowing with slaver. Its claws clicked upon the tile floor and it hurled itself toward me, beating me down with its own terrible eyes. The word that popped into my head was Jackal.

And as soon as the beast reared itself from behind the corner, a whole pack of others followed in its wake, snarling and skidding upon the floor as they moved to turn, stumbling upon each other and scrambling toward me. Six more. There were seven dogs come to tear me apart. I couldn't move for terror; my knees threatened to buckle. I couldn't even think.

I could only watch as the barking, snarling, and screaming faded from my ears. I suddenly could hear nothing at all. Not even my own heart beat. And then a feint voice filled my head. *I will take your hearing, and you will not be afraid.* And suddenly I wasn't. Something came over me so extraordinarily, some warmth in a rush of peace, and I wasn't. I swallowed and oddly enough squatted on my heels toward the level of the dogs' eyes, which still glared at me with a passionate hunger I knew would never be sated. I held up my hand.

The first dog—the largest and fiercest and most likely the alpha—skidded to a halt two inches from my hand and only a few more from my face. It barked once and the other six behind it skidded to a halt much farther behind the two of us. I stared into the Jackal's eyes, aware of its snarling fangs and the strings of thick, foaming saliva that slinked to the floor like syrup. And then I spoke.

I had no idea what I said, only that my lips moved and that I still heard nothing. And that I still was not afraid. I said things I didn't even know I knew, my mouth working over and over. The Jackal's eyes were locked onto my own and my hand never left its position closely set between our faces. An extraordinary sense of power filled me, knowing somehow that this dog would abide by my will and my words. I felt that power flow through my hand and my throat, and I did not stop. After mere, harsh moments, the Jackal closed its mouth, licked its muzzle, and retreated, squealing and whining away from me. The others followed it, slipping on the smooth tile floor and falling over each other, skidding away as fast as they could.

I took a moment to breathe myself, then

stood slowly from my crouch. I saw the maids standing there, gathered far around me and staring, but I paid them no heed. I turned toward the staircase and watched the girl sitting there. The sight still disgusted me, but I faced it now. The voice filled my head again.

I have chosen you for this. Satan has entered this place of innocence, and you are here to drive him out. This I could not believe. I shook my head vigorously, unable to take my eyes off of the girl. It couldn't be. I was no one to do this, no one to perform miracles!

I am the wrong person for this, I thought. *I do not have this power. Choose someone else!* I was scared out of my mind and I dare not move to do what I realized I had been sent here to do.

I have chosen *you. It is your time,* the voice continued, and I knew, without a doubt, that this was a necessity. I could not alter the course of my purpose, and without doing this, I would never leave this place. I could not ever let this go. I was here for an exorcism.

I fingered the silver cross still hanging at my throat, now feeling the power and guidance that it gave and that it had lacked for so long. Now was my time. I thrust open the double doors, and walked toward the horrifying girl on the stairs, this time devoid of the fear of her. She looked up at me, branding my soul with those eyes, and then she, like the Jackals, began to snarl. I stepped closer, achingly placing each foot on the step above, and held my hand out to her. She wrenched forward to snap at my fingers. Her forehead brushed against my thumb and she reeled back against the stairs, howling in pain. A burn mark lay upon her skin in the shape of my thumb, and she only snarled at me more. I now knew what power I held in my fingers alone.

I pressed my whole hand to her head, feeling her skin sizzle and boil at my touch, and I spoke. My lips moved again, without sound and without recognition, and I stared at her, burning her. Her limbs flailed in all directions as she shook her head wildly to get beyond my touch. Many times she struggled away, clawing at me and biting and screaming. But then I finally gained a sturdy hold upon her half-burnt face, muttering those strange words. She could not get away now. And with each soundless thing that flowed from my lips, I felt myself growing weaker, losing my sight. My breath stuck in my throat, and I soon lost the feeling in my hand altogether. All my strength flowed into the act. But I held her tighter.

With one final screech, the girl lunged

backward, her back arching, and fell limp upon the stairs—lifeless, motionless. I sighed, peeling my hand from her charred skin, and slowly climbed down the staircase. I staggered out of the double doors, letting them swing behind me, and made my way further—anywhere further from that place.

I couldn't hold myself up any longer; I had no strength left. And so I collapsed upon the cold tile with my arm bent uncomfortably behind me. But I had no want to move it. I could hardly keep my eyes open. I glanced around and saw the maids still standing there, some with hands over their mouths, others wide-eyed with shock and terror. But what did they know? I sighed again and dropped my head.

I lay there for what seemed like hours, feeling a fish out of water. My hearing slowly drained back into my head, and then I heard the two doors swing open behind me. I dragged myself around to see. There stood the little girl, no longer the host for the evil I had so trodden out. Her hair fell in clean curls, coddling her face and hanging over her shoulders. The dress was no longer a horror to behold, now clean and shining and everything a little girl should love to wear. Her face had color again, the healthy, glowing pink color of her soul, no doubt, and blue eyes stared out at me. A small smile cracked her lips, and she placed a tiny, pudgy, clean hand to her heart. I could not help but smile back.

My eyelids were burdensome cement bricks on my face, and I stopped trying to lift them. I had always viewed my life as worthless— a life without God and without hope. Without something to live for. Now I understood why I had not spent my energy on the normal sparks of life, why I had chosen, after all, not to end it years ago. It was done. And I had done well.

About Kathrin Hutson

Kathrin's latest Fantasy novel 'Daughter of the Drackan', the first in the 'Gyenona's Children' series, was published earlier this year and is available on Amazon and through most ebook outlets.

In addition to writing exquisitely dark fiction, Kathrin runs her own independent editing company, KLH CreateWorks, for Indie Authors of all genres. She also serves as Story Coordinator and Chief Editor for Collaborative Writing Challenge, and Editing Director for Rambunctious

The Grim Keepers

Rambling Press, Inc. Needless to say, she doesn't have time to do anything she doesn't enjoy.

Kathrin keeps a vast collection of single earrings (and wears them), has fulfilled her dream of naming one of her dogs Brucewillis, and can't remember the last time she didn't laugh at one of her own jokes.

www.kathrinhutsonfiction.com
www.facebook.com/kathrinhutsonfiction
www.klhcreateworks.com
www.facebook.com/klhcreateworks
Twitter: @KlhCreateWorks

The Grim Keepers

Annie's Fetch
By Virginia Carraway Stark

Annie stood on the rotted boards of the back porch. Her red hair was faded and threaded with white. She was deadheading blossoms from a fading rose bush and humming under her breath. A breeze crept under her woven shawl and ruffled her skirt and hair. She shivered and clutched her shoulders, looking around with wide blue eyes. Her house was older, but all her own. Wind chimes decorated the rowan trees and eavestroughing, and marbles had been placed into holes in the fence and balcony to let in little dreams of light. The rest of the wall was made of slats covered in plaster that had been exposed by the tar paper over it. Sid had left without finishing the siding, and with only the tar paper to protect her and Felicity, the heating bills were high, and there were still shivering nights where all the sweaters and blankets couldn't protect against the icy fingers eating into the house.

Those fingers weren't here now, but there was something else in the wind, a deep and resentful feeling of betrayal and hatred that reminded her of the days before her divorce. Those days of fear, regret, and violence tightened around her throat like a noose. Annie lifted one of the terracotta pots to check if the Artemisia was ready for more water. A movement under the pot got her attention and she delicately peered under the herb. A wolf spider was curled up on the bottom. One of its hairy legs was unable to hide from the edge of the pot, and it jerked it out of sight and looked up at where Annie's pale face looked down at him.

She wasn't normally scared of spiders, but the cognizance in this one sent a shiver down her spine. It seemed to be aware of her in an above-average sort of way, even for a larger spider. Should she kill it? It was a dilemma for a gardener. The wolf spider would destroy a lot of her enemies, and certainly under the Artemisia like that he was a force for good? She looked at him again, craning her neck to see around the bottom of the pot.

The spider darted out from its hiding place near the drain hole and latched onto Annie's finger. She threw the pot across the deck where it broke into brown shards, and black soil sprayed across the little gardening area. The spider reared its front legs at her. Annie let out a cry and tried to hit it onto the balcony ledge, but the wolf spider chewed deeper into her finger. She started to really panic now, and she pulled at it with her other hand. It flailed its hairy front legs at her and finally let go, dropping between two boards on the deck before she could get any revenge.

Annie backed into the house, closing the door behind her. She was regretting the gap between the door and jam. That thing could slide between the loose edges of the jam easily enough. The sense that someone had sent it settled into her heart. It was Sid. He had sent the spider. He always loved the creepy crawly things or the things with fangs and claws. She remembered one night he had brought one such animal into the bedroom; that was the last night for her. The night she took measures and got him out of her life once and for all.

The screen door had caught in the sudden

chill wind and was blowing back and forth.

Creak. Slam. Creak. Slam-slam-slam.

"Mama, the screen door is blowing." Annie grabbed her daughter to her as the small girl walked towards the door.

"I know, sweetheart. Let's just let it blow." Annie kissed the blonde-red curls on her daughter's head. Even in her hair the scent of autumn had suddenly permeated.

"Is it winter yet?" Felicity asked.

Annie felt a chill in her heart. "Not winter, not yet. Go back to your coloring, sweetie. Don't go outside unless you ask first. Promise?"

Felicity nodded and kissed Annie's cheek. She ran back to her coloring and Annie went back to the window. Annie's finger was throbbing. The venom from the wolf spider wasn't deadly, but it made her finger swell; the spider had really savaged her skin and bits of flesh stuck up in miniature. Some of her blood fell to the floor, staining the scrubbed, nearly-white hardwood.

Creak-slam-slam. Creak-creak-slam.

SLAM.

Annie jumped, her long fingers curling into tense fists around her shawl. The shawl felt good against the bite and staunched up the blood. She should go rinse it out but all she could do was stare and think. This was wrong. She watched the yellowed leaves on the black birch that dominated her back lawn. They rapidly landed on her lawn and drifted into the flower bed. Her eyes went unfocused and her lips moved. Syllables, barely heard, escaped her mouth. Felicity stopped coloring to watch her mother. Annie had the sight and Felicity was showing signs of it as well. Annie murmured a prayer, not one from her catechisms; this was one her great grandmother had taught her.

"Amen," said Felicity at the end. Annie turned to Felicity and smiled.

"Amen," she agreed. They shared a loving glance, then both jumped at the sudden knock on the door. Annie smoothed her hair that had a gift for flying out of its constraints even when there wasn't an evil wind blowing.

She opened the door and a gust of wind blew the inner door out of her fingers and slammed it into the plaster walls. Standing on the other side of the door was herself, or something very like herself. "My fetch," Annie mumbled in recognition of the spirit. She had been told as a young girl that this spirit signified your death or near death.

She looked eerily like Annie, but her skin

was pale and blue and her eyes were rimmed in red. She wore a white nightgown and looked wet. Her bare feet left damp footprints for only a few steps behind her, and her cloudy blue eyes looked up to meet Annie's gaze before she smiled. Her smile was filled with pointed, yellowed teeth, and was as malignant as the cancer that had killed Annie's mother.

Annie tried to scream but only a whimper came out. She took a step back and the thing, the demon that looked like a fell mirror, took a step towards her. The hem of her nightgown now dripped water, and as she swayed the smallest of drops fell, helped by a gust of wind, inside the threshold of Annie's home.

Annie jumped away from the water droplet and fumbled for the door. The fetch slowly raised its foot to take another shambling step towards her. Annie slammed the door and threw the deadbolt.

Creak-creak. Slam. Slam-slam-creak. No one was there now. The back porch was empty except for the drying footprints that led up to the door and then vanished.

The wind blew harder now. It cackled down the painted white bricks of the chimney and gusted ashes across the room. Annie wanted to rush to Felicity and scoop her up in her arms but didn't want to touch her. She felt sick to her stomach and tainted from the thing that had worn her face. She didn't want to spread the taint.

"Sweetheart, mama's going to take a shower."

Felicity nodded gravely. "Can I color in the bathroom?"

"Of course, that's a great idea." Annie waited for Felicity to gather her crayons up but didn't help or take her daughter's hand. The little girl was only five, but she had seen the fetch too. She didn't know what it meant, but she knew what it felt like: death.

By the time Annie had showered and gotten into her pajamas she felt okay to give Felicity a hug. She went back to the bathroom, after reassuring herself that Felicity was still safe, and gave her finger a proper sterilization, wrapping it in a band-aid. Her entire hand was numb and swollen. Annie grabbed Felicity after tending her hand and pulled her onto the couch to cover her in kisses and hugs. She was still hugging her daughter when she heard the little girl's belly growl angrily. Annie rolled her eyes at herself.

"We forgot to eat!" Annie exclaimed

"Well, I know that," Felicity said, a little

grouchy about it. Felicity tended to have a better memory for the things of life like eating and schedules than Annie had ever managed to develop.

"I can tell you know that. Your tummy knows it too. Let me make it up to you in the form of a surprise pizza night."

Felicity nodded emphatic agreement and squeezed her mom in a bigger hug. They didn't have a lot of money and pizza night was the biggest special treat they had.

It took about a week for the feel of that evil presence to fade and even when it did fade, Annie still glanced up nervously anytime the wind blew the screen door open or she saw anything that might be a spider. Nothing happened, and the next morning made the bad night and the ominous feelings seem like bad dreams, or as though they had just spooked themselves. The only thing that remained was the spider bite, and that had decided to settle into an uncomfortable boil.

Other things were on Annie's mind right now, however. When Annie got distracted by concerns, Felicity grew sensitive as well. She knew Annie sometimes went through hard times, sadness plaguing her along with a lack of funds, and dealing with the small town prejudices that were so easily directed towards a mother who 'couldn't hold her man'.

Other things came up as well, the sorts of things impossible for a single mother without a peck of child support coming in to ignore. The car insurance was late and the next day the car wouldn't start at all. They needed firewood right away, too. The nights were getting cold and Annie didn't make enough money cleaning houses and giving people card readings and love philters to pay for natural gas for the furnace.

She decided the firewood and new shoes for Felicity would have to take top priority. They would just have to walk until they had a bit of good luck. Lately, the only luck they seemed to have was the other kind. The next day the autumn weather seemed to have been dispelled and a gasp of summer came back, along with a change in Annie's luck.

Usually, Annie walked Felicity to and from kindergarten each day, but business had finally picked up again and the client was paying well for her many questions that she wanted 'Lady Annie', as they called her around town, to answer for her. Annie would have enough by tomorrow to have the car fixed, and she could worry about insurance afterwards. Felicity knew the way home and she would know that if her mama wasn't waiting for her, it was likely for this exact reason. The bad humor of Fort Fraser seemed to have dispersed towards Annie and Felicity again, and the recalcitrant to pay some money for Annie's many eclectic services.

Annie put away the deck of tarot cards and her client put an extra couple of dollars on the table. "Thank you so much, Annie."

Annie smiled wanly. "I wish it could have been better news."

"I'm content with it. I had suspicions. I'm glad to finally know." Rita hugged Lady Annie and kissed her on the cheek.

Annie closed the door behind her and wiped an errant tear from her cheek. She had drawn a spare care for herself while Rita was in the washroom, the presence of the fetch hadn't left her life. In fact, the time drew near when she would face it; she would look her own death in the eyes. Annie noticed that Rita had forgotten her purse on the edge of her chair.

She heard footsteps on the deck and went to open the door, grabbing Rita's purse on her way. She must have realized she had forgotten it before she got out to the car. She heard the sound of a car door and an engine start. It sounded like Rita's car. Then who was at the door?

She had the door partly open and started to shut it without checking to see who knocked, but a long-fingered, white-skinned hand inserted itself before she had the chance.

"Sid! What are you doing here?" Annie exclaimed as she caught a glimpse of the dark, dead eyes on the other side of the door. His eyes were as cold and passionless as they had always been. He put a shiny black boot into the door so she couldn't try to close it again and Annie heard a small voice.

"Mama. Let me in, Mama!"

Felicity's wrist was clutched tightly in Sid's other hand. Her cheeks were streaked with tears and Annie could see she had a black eye coming up.

"Let me in, Annie. If you leave me out on the deck with only Felicity to keep me company, I'm going to have nothing to do except come up with some nasty ways to amuse myself. You wouldn't want our daughter to see what I'm capable of, do you, sweetheart?" He smiled at Annie, his teeth long and pointed. She could call the police, but he might run off with Felicity if she did, or worse. He hadn't come back since Felicity had been a baby and Annie had enacted a spell to banish him from their life for good.

Now he was back. What had changed?

"Mama, please, he's hurting me." Felicity had never known her father and now she faced the monster.

Annie stepped away from the door and let Sid and Felicity in. She grabbed Felicity and picked her up and held her away from Sid, who smirked at her. Annie couldn't think of how he had found her again after all these years. Sid sauntered through the house as though he still owned it. She had a restraining order against him; the last time he had been here he had cut Annie and threatened the baby. It was the police who had removed him from the house but it was her magic that kept him away after his brief time in jail.

"You haven't changed a bit, Annie. You're still completely do-able. I've been watching you, you know. I'm surprised you don't have some new 'boy' in your life."

"I don't want anyone. I don't want you, Sid. Please leave." Annie's voice was quiet and tremulous, her eyes averted; it felt as though the years of freedom had never been. He was back and in control. "Why did you come now?"

He smiled his sick, dead smile and

caressed Felicity's cheek. "I remembered that I had a little girl. I came for her. She has a right to know her daddy."

Annie slid Felicity to the floor and the little girl ran from the room. Annie watched Sid's gaze follow their daughter. She took him by the hand. Why was it so cold?

He looked up at her touch and took her into his arms. Annie complied, her smile stiff on her cheeks. Looking behind him, she saw a trail of wet boot marks. His arms were damp around her too. He whispered in her ear and his breath was chill and smelled like rotten fish and algae. "I have come to take our daughter home. You've had her long enough."

"You can't have her. She's not yours. The courts—"

"The courts don't matter. Don't be stupider than usual, Annie. Nothing the mortal world can do can hurt me now. I told you I would find the most powerful forces and I did. I found them, and I became them. Let me take our daughter and I will fill her with the same power. She will become magnificent."

Annie shivered in his arms. "She's mine. You abandoned her and you have no rights."

"I abandoned her, but then she started to

call for me at night. 'Daddy, who are you?', 'Daddy I love you,', 'Daddy, please...come home." He imitated her familiar voice cruelly, making her sweetness insipid even to Annie's ear.

"She didn't know what she was asking for."

"Well, she will have eternity to find out." He grinned his shark smile and Annie gagged on his fetid breath.

Felicity had been asking more questions about who her father had been. Part of it was from hearing rumors about him around school, but a larger part was that she was a little girl who wanted to know her father. Annie realized she should have paid more attention to the questions, but now it was too late. Felicity came back into the room. Sid dropped Annie on the couch with a force that pushed the breath out of her lungs. It wasn't just the physical movement, it was the disdain in him, the hatred. He grabbed Felicity up as quick as a viper. He kissed her cheek, a slow, lingering kiss from his cold, dead lips. Felicity recoiled from him but his arms held her tightly and her squirming just made him smile more.

Annie sat up. She was weak and trembling from being touched by him, flung by him. She found her voice with some difficulty.

The Grim Keepers

"Please, Sid, it wasn't her who called you. It was me."

Her face was as pale as a mask and her lips were dry and cold. Annie could hardly force the words out of her mouth,

He turned, his face open with desire. He wanted Felicity, true, but he longed for Annie even more. Lady Annie with her special gifts. If he could take her with him he would be more powerful in the realm of rot and death than ever before. He dropped Felicity to the ground. Her legs shook and she crawled behind the couch, crying and moaning. Even his touch was pain.

"You want to come with my at long last, Lady Annie? You swear you will come with me? You swear you will be my bride once more?"

"I will swear so long as you leave Felicity alone forever. Renounce her as your daughter and I will be your bride, Sid."

Sid held his hand out towards where Felicity hid behind the couch. "Felicity Dunworth, I renounce you now and for all time as my daughter."

His other hand didn't let go of Lady Annie for a moment. He turned to her, his eyes reflecting nothing but the image of Annie's own face as he leaned forward to kiss her. She saw her eyes were rimmed with red and devoid of all hope and life. Her face was thin and her own eyes frightened her. The white dress she had worn for the reading was soaked through with damp moisture from her husband. The fetch had come to her and embraced her. She turned to say one last goodbye to Felicity, but she saw their wet footprints ended abruptly behind them at a wall. On the wall was a picture of an old deck covered in the leaves of autumn, and a redheaded woman with white threaded through her hair, tending her potted Artemisia and clutching her shawl against a sudden, cruel wind. Annie reached her fingers out behind her and saw they were draped with seaweed. She cried out Felicity's name, but in this underwater realm of dead dreams, her sobs were only bubbles of air that popped soundlessly when they reached the surface.

About Virginia Caraway Stark

Virginia Carraway Stark has a diverse portfolio and has been writing professionally for nearly a decade. Getting an early start on writing, Virginia has had a gift for communication, oration, and storytelling from an early age. Over the years she has developed this into a wide range of products, from screenplays to novels, articles, blogging, and travel journalism. She works with other writers, artists, and poets to hone her talents and to offer encouragement and insight to others. She has been an honorable mention at Canne Film Festival for her screenplay "Blind Eye", and was nominated for an Aurora Award.

http://www.virginiastark.wordpress.com
https://m.facebook.com/Virginiacarrawaystark?ref=bookmarks

Bollywog
By Sharon Flood

The Fergusons' garden of rotting vegetation and dark, damp soil stretched out for an acre behind their centuries-old, black, field-stone house. It cast a brooding, early-evening shadow over a group of girls who prepared to set up camp in the meadow behind the garden.

"Here's a good flat patch of dirt where we can pitch dad's old fishing trip tent, girls. It's huge. All ten of us will be able to fit our sleeping bags in it," Sharla Ferguson said.

One of the girls stooped, picked up a fistful of black earth, and smelled it.

"This dirt smells burnt, Sharla. Was there a fire here?" she asked.

"Yeah. Over fifty years ago. There was

some kind of grass fire. Nothing has grown on this patch since. I don't know why. Dad told me that he and his friend, Felix, dug up some ancient artifacts and some charred human remains here years ago, before I was born."

"Eww," was the general reaction among the girls. Sharla grinned and shrugged. The ringtone on her cell phone sent out a shrill whistle, and everyone jumped. She laughed and answered it. She listened for a moment, said, "Okay," and hung up.

"Dad says it's getting late, and if we want the tent we have to go get it now. He doesn't want to set it up in the dark. Let's go," she said.

She headed up the path through the garden with her nine friends trailing behind her. The late autumn day was overcast and gray. A hint of winter in the stiff, cool breeze blew dead leaves around the girls' feet. There was a good deal of grumbling as the girls trudged through the muck of the path. Andrea Lawler strode up beside Sharla and kept pace with her.

"It's almost sundown, Sharla. My new sneakers are wet and filthy, and I'm tired and hungry. It could be full dark before we set up the tent. Can't we do this tomorrow? It's Halloween. We could go trick-or-treating."

The Grim Keepers

"It's my thirteenth birthday, Andrea. I'm the last one of us to become a teenager. We all agreed we were too old to go out on Halloween night. Everyone loved the idea of having a camping-out sleepover—including you."

"I changed my mind."

"Oh, you're such a whiner," Sharla snapped as she quickened her step and forged ahead of the others. She wondered why she was suddenly so cranky. She liked Andrea.

The group finally made it to the old carriage house that had been converted to a garage and machine shed for seasonal equipment. Sharla's dad, Gary, led the way. The stone building was over two hundred years old, the remnants of a country estate that had dwindled down to the house, the carriage house, and five acres. Now, a double overhead garage door stood where the wide open area for the carriages used to be. When they all arrived in front of the doors, Gary tried to open it with the remote. Nothing happened. He tried the manual keypad on a side doorpost, and the door opened about a foot, then stopped. He tried to pull it up, but nothing happened.

"It won't budge. I'll need help, I think. Gather 'round ladies. Pick a spot, get a grip on the door, and we'll count to three, then we'll all lift up at once."

The girls assembled along the width of the door, squatted, and put their hands under the door. Gary began the count.

"One, two, three…lift."

Shrieks of terror shattered the silence as the doors rolled up and a huge black cloud of bats descended upon the girls.

"Ah! Bats—I hate bats!"

Sharla ran back away from the doors. She bumped into several of her panicking friends who were also running away.

Gary leaned against the doorpost, laughing as he focused his camcorder on the stampeding girls. Some of the bats landed on them and were flung away as the girls ran. Sharla stomped on several bats before she realized they were awfully flat. She picked one up by its mangled wingtip and yelled at her friends.

"Andrea, Joanie, Lisa, Allison, Colleen, come back. They're only paper."

She went to join her friends, carrying several of the black construction paper origami bats. The cleverly created three-dimensional flying rodents were examined carefully, as if they might suddenly come to life and take flight. Sharla stalked back to her father.

The Grim Keepers

"Dad. That was not funny. "

"It wasn't supposed to be funny. It's Halloween. It's supposed to be scary. This year's video is going to be the best yet. You're thirteen now. I thought you'd be harder to scare, so I had to come up with something really special that you would never suspect."

"Well, you got me, as well as my friends. Are you happy now? You can play your stupid video for the whole family tomorrow and laugh at how you scared the crap out of all of us."

Sharla enjoyed the annual Halloween stunts that her dad had always staged for her and her friends. Those had been a little bit scary, but mostly funny. This one had actually scared her. She was not pleased.

Gary grinned as he watched Sharla's friends giggle while they threw the paper bats at each other.

"Still mad at me, Punkin?" Gary leaned over and gave her a quick kiss on the forehead. Sharla shrugged and grinned.

"No, I guess not. It was a really good stunt, Dad. It's going to be all over school on Monday. Are you done now? Can we get that tent and set it up, please?"

"Okay, but help me clean up the bats first."

The Grim Keepers

Gary went into the carriage house and brought out a package of large leaf bags. The girls had a good time playing "throw the bats in the bag" as Gary held the bags open to receive the paper missiles.

When they finished, Gary led the group up the narrow, creaky stairs to the loft of the old carriage house, which used to hold harnesses, traces, and other trappings required for carriages and the horses that pulled them. It was now used for storage.

There were squeals of disgust as spider webs and mouse droppings were unearthed during the search through all the old furniture and decades of stored junk. The carriage house was built long before electricity, so some rudimentary electrical wiring had been installed sometime in the middle of the twentieth century. A low wattage lightbulb hung from a porcelain lamp holder, screwed to an overhead beam in the middle of the loft.

Gary eventually found the old steamer trunk in which the big canvas tent had always been kept. There was a large, old padlock on the brass hasp, but it was unlocked with the key still in it. He took the lock off and put it in his pocket, then lifted the rounded top. The girls gathered around the open trunk and reached into it to grab handfuls of the canvas. Sharla pulled out a heavy object and held it up toward the dim light.

"Hey, look what I found. It's an antique cast-iron carriage lamp. It was right in there with the tent. You must have taken it on your last camping trip. How long ago was that, Dad?"

"Thirteen years ago today, actually. You mother wasn't due to have you for another two weeks, so we went up to the Great North Woods for an international fishing derby. There were hundreds of sportsmen in boats all over a small, secluded lake vying for the grand prize. It was a twenty-four-foot fishing cabin cruiser with two live fish wells, six rod holders, and a fully equipped kitchen. It was worth five-thousand dollars."

Gary's mind drifted back to that long-ago fishing trip and to the fishing boat they could have won if they'd been willing to claim the huge, dead fish which drifted ashore right below their campsite. If it wasn't for the gruesome baggage it carried along with it…

Gary gasped as the full memory of that night assaulted his mind in a rush of fear and revulsion. He jumped up from his kneeling position on the floor where he'd been pulling out the canvas, grabbed the lamp out of Sharla's hand, and threw it into the trunk. There were several shouts of protest and surprise as Gary pulled the tent out of the girls' hands, bundled it up and shoved it back in the trunk. He pushed it down with his feet so he could get the lid closed. He took the padlock out of his pocket and put it through the brass hasp on the trunk. He walked over to one end of it and squatted to get his hands underneath.

"Girls, help me lift this on its end," he told them gruffly. "Sharla, go get that thick logging chain hanging from the rafter over there, and bring it to me."

"Why? What's going on, Daddy?" Sharla gasped, frightened.

"Don't argue, Sharla Diane, just go get the chain."

Sharla let out another little gasp. Her dad was a gentle man; he rarely raised his voice to her. His harsh tone surprised her, particularly since she hadn't done anything wrong. Holding back tears, Sharla ran to get the chain. By the time she got back, the girls and Gary had upended the trunk. He wound the chain around it as many time as could, unlocked the padlock, put it through the two ends of the chain, then locked it again. With a grunt, he pushed it back flat on the floor.

"All right, girls, let's get out of here," he said. "Now!" he roared when they hesitated.

There was a general stampede down the stairs and out to the driveway, which was now awash with the last pale rays of sunset. Gary joined them.

"D-does this mean my sleepover is canceled, Daddy?" Sharla asked as her voice broke and her bottom lip quivered.

Gary's manner softened when he saw the effect his bizarre behavior had on his only child. He walked over to her and put his arm around her shoulders.

"Of course not, Punkin. You've been planning this for weeks. I'll call Patricia Kairne, your Girl Scout leader. I'm sure she'll lend us one of the tents your troop used to go camping this summer."

"What's wrong with this tent, Dad?"

"It's old, and it's been folded up for years. Your friends have already noticed how musty it smells. You saw the mouse droppings around it. There are probably nests of mice in it."

"Oh...okay..." Sharla agreed, bewildered. This weird behavior just wasn't like her dad at all.

"Why don't all of you go into the house for

snacks while I go get the troop tent? Sharla's mom put out quite a spread in the dining room."

The girls obeyed quietly and headed for the house.

As soon as the group was out of sight, Gary took his cell phone out of his back pocket. He dialed a number that he knew well from years of Sharla being in the Girl Scouts.

"Hello, Pat? It's Gary Ferguson here. Could we borrow one of your troop tents for tonight? Sharla is having a sleepover. Yes, I know it's short notice, but the tent we were counting on is rotted clear through one side. It was badly stored in a damp area. It's completely unusable," Gary lied. "Good, I'll be around by the troop clubhouse in about an hour. Thanks a lot, Pat, I really appreciate it."

Gary hung up and speed-dialed his neighbor and best buddy, Felix Hauptman. He tapped his foot impatiently on the grass as he waited for his friend to answer.

"Hi, Felix. Can you come by the house right away? I need to get rid of an old steamer trunk. Yeah, that one. The one with the tent in it."

Gary held the phone away from his ear as loud profanity issued out of the receiver.

"I know I was supposed to get rid of it, but

the minute I had it stored in the carriage house, Maggie from next door ran over. She had seen me pull up, and she came to tell me that her husband, Carl, took Arlene to the hospital with labor pains."

Gary listened to Felix's response.

"After Sharla was born, I forgot all about it. Nothing ever happened in the thirteen years since it's been in there, so I think nothing will happen now. We'll take it out to that old dump down Zuwicki road and burn the thing, just to make sure. After we're done, we have to go around by Sharla's scout clubhouse. We have to pick up a troop tent for her sleepover."

He was just about to hang up when Felix continued the conversation.

"I know. I shouldn't have even agreed to use the tent in the first place, but Sharla saw it in several pictures from our old camping days. She asked me if I still had it, and I said yes. She automatically took that as an agreement to use it. She only asked me to dig it out this morning. I had already opened it when I remembered about that night. Well, there seems to be no harm done. We'll get rid of it, and that'll be that."

When Felix arrived with his truck, he backed it up to the lawn in front of the carriage house. If he had gotten any closer to the closed garage door, he would have buckled it. He jumped out and ran around the back to open the tailgate. Then he joined Gary, who stood a little bit off to the side.

"Where's the trunk?"

"Still up in the loft. I couldn't handle it myself, and the less those girls have to do with that trunk, the better."

"All right, then. Let's go get this over with."

Gary went over to the keypad and opened the overhead doors. The two men ran up the narrow stairs and over to the trunk.

"You take this handle, I'll take the other, and we'll haul this thing out of here."

Gary nodded. They each grabbed the leather handle bolted on each end. With a mighty grunt of effort, both men picked up the trunk and headed down the narrow stairs. It was a tight fit, but they finally managed to get it to the bottom. They carried it to the truck and hauled it up into the back.

They pushed it to the side where a steel bar and several leather straps waited to safely secure the trunk. They strapped the trunk down and jumped back down to the ground. After Felix closed the tailgate, they both got in and drove away. Neither one spoke until they reached their destination.

Felix turned down the mostly overgrown Zuwicki road. There was nothing on it but the old dump, and it had been closed for years. When they reached the unused landfill, Gary jumped out and used his bolt cutters to cut the rusted chain that held the metal gate closed. He swung it wide open and hopped back in the truck.

They drove along the barely visible track to the dumping site. When they got there, both men got out and lowered the tailgate. They released the trunk and pushed it onto the gate. When both of them were on the ground, they pulled the trunk down and carried it to a flat spot overrun with vegetation. Felix retrieved the can of gasoline he had also strapped to the side. He unceremoniously poured the entire contents onto the trunk and lit it. The resulting fireball shot several meters into the air above it. Thick smoke billowed into the sky.

"Holy shit!" Gary screamed as he felt the heat of the instant bonfire. "Are you nuts, Felix? That smoke's going to be seen for miles."

"If it is, then it is. It'll be blamed on Halloween pranksters."

They stood there and stared at the fire,

mesmerized, neither one making a move to leave.

"This will be the end of it for good, then," Gary remarked as he watched the dancing flames.

"There should have been an end to it thirteen years ago," Felix said peevishly. The longer he stood there, the more he wanted to leave, but he couldn't even move.

"My wife was giving birth. I never even thought about getting rid of the tent."

"I'm not talking about keeping it. I mean we should have burnt it where it was."

"There were fishermen all up and down the river. That big a fire would have brought somebody running. We should never have gone up there anyway, so close to Arlene's due date. You were so greedy for that grand prize you couldn't even think straight."

"It would have been fine if you hadn't dragged along that stupid carriage lamp, Gary."

"I didn't know it was in the trunk with the tent. I thought we might be able to use it. I was just cleaning the glass to see if there was still any oil in it when that…that thing just appeared out of nowhere. Remember how pissed off it was when you called it a genie?" Gary chuckled a little in spite of the horror of it all.

"That's right," Felix laughed. "It puffed up

its chest and floated in a cloud of black smoke above us."

"You call me a genie. You think I am a genie with its paltry three wishes? I can do your bidding as many times as you like, it told us," Gary remembered.

"You didn't have to take it up on its offer, Felix. Why did you, anyway? You could tell it was pure evil just by looking at it. I was terrified down to my bones."

"You know why. I wanted it to bring us the biggest fish in the river to win the derby. We could have shared the brand new fishing boat prize between us. I had no way of knowing that the thing was homicidal."

"You're right, you couldn't have known that, or that the biggest fish had already been caught by a guy further down the lake."

Gary shivered at the sudden image that entered unbidden into his head—the wide, staring eyes of the gray, waterlogged body that drifted up to shore right below their campsite. He could only have been in the water for a few hours since the derby entry number was still pinned to his shirt, but it looked like he was already decomposing.

The trunk burned steadily as Gary and Felix went over the nightmare that they had lived through thirteen years ago. Gary sat on a rock and Felix made himself comfortable on a clump of grass nearby.

"We should have at least let someone know where the poor guy was. It took two days for the searchers to find him. Everybody assumed that the huge Muskie pulled him overboard and he drowned. He was still clutching his fishing pole with the fish on the end of it when they found him," Gary remarked thoughtfully as he watched the fire.

"If you hadn't panicked and trapped the thing inside the tent, we could have used it to do stuff for us all these years. I wish I still had him to do my bidding."

"Maybe, but at what expense? You know that whatever we wished for, someone else would pay with their lives."

"We don't know that for sure, Gary. If we were specific enough, we could get around that. I just wish you hadn't pulled the tent down on it and smashed it repeatedly with a rock."

As they talked, they had turned away from the fire, so they didn't notice that the smoke had taken on a sinister shape all it's own.

"It is as you bid, master."

Both men screamed in horror as the evil

thing floated over to Felix.

"You're dead, you're gone. Go away," Felix yelled.

"I am *Bollywog*. I cannot die. I merely slept because you made no further biddings of me."

"Well, then, I wish you gone somewhere else—the bottom of the ocean, forever."

"If you so desire, but you did say earlier that you wish you still had me to do your bidding. That wish predates this wish. First come, first served."

"Hold that thought. I'll get back to you."

Felix turned around and looked for his friend. He wasn't there.

"Where is Gary?"

"He was very astute in assuming that every wish you make is paid for…by someone else."

The Bollywog nodded toward the trunk, its burning lid still wide-open. Gary lay crumpled up in the trunk. His head hung over the side where a gaping wound in his throat dripped his life's blood onto the smoldering coals of his funeral pyre. Felix fainted in terror. The fire crept along the ground and set Felix's clothing alight. He woke up from his faint just in time to feel the agony of the consuming fire.

The Grim Keepers

***

Three days later, Sharla sat up in bed, crying her heart out. The truck had been found at the dump but with no sign of Gary and Felix. The whole town had been out searching for them ever since. She just couldn't believe that her dad had abandoned her without a word of goodbye. She got up to go to the bathroom and she tripped over something in the dark. She turned the light on and discovered the old, iron carriage lamp that had been up in the loft. For some unknown reason, she sat down and picked it up. She hugged it to her chest.

"I want my Daddy back!" she wailed.

A thick black cloud of smoke formed above her head.

About Sharon Flood

Sharon was born and raised in the St. Lawrence River Valley in the 1,000 Islands region. She graduated from grade 13 in Thousand Islands Secondary School in Brockville and began writing in high school. Her talent lay dormant until many years later she discovered protagonize.com in 2008. Making contacts and collaborating here led to publishing a time travel anthology.

The Grim Keepers

Sharon is recognized as a Mob Boss at Masquerade Crew, having acquired this title through her many book reviews.

After working forty years in retail, Sharon is now retired and has more free time to do what she loves most—reading and writing.

http://www.protagonize.com/author/moonwalker
http://www.amazon.com/Forevermore-Travel-Anthology-Sharon-Flood-ebook/dp/B00XSBH4UW
http://www.masqueradecrew.com/p/the-masquerade-mob.html

The Grim Keepers

Cherry Oak Road
By Laura Callender

Two butterflies danced provocatively across the cloud-cast sky. A streetlamp illuminated their impressive designs, a momentary distraction from my daily walk home. Autumn was not my favorite month. I loved the colors as the leaves started to turn from a vibrant green to a burnt, delicate brown, but had come to hate the promise of a brutal winter knocking at my door.

This neighborhood gave me the creeps. I walked along the same tree-lined path for almost a year now, but still felt a shiver crawl up my spine every single time. All the houses sat back off the street behind cascading lawns. Each remained proud on its own plot, looking down at me with

The Grim Keepers

vacant gloom. My realtor had told me something bad had happened on this street, and although the houses were solid, they now did not appeal to anyone who did their research.

One house in particular grabbed my attention, it sat a bit closer to the road than the rest. I was sure I just saw someone inside, a man stood at the window. I had to crease my eyes and tilt my head slightly to be sure, but decided it was nothing.

Locals had petitioned many times over the years to allow developers in to make use of the land, but the law prevented it. These houses were owned by not one but six families, one for each respective house. As yet, no one could be traced to change those laws.

I lived just one block from this street, and financially benefitted from having to endure this daily walk to the station. There was another route, but it added ten minutes to my four minute journey. After a long day, those extra ten minutes could be a killer.

I didn't care for old ghost stories and really didn't listen to idle gossip, so I figured learning more about Cherry Oak road could wait until a rainy day.

The Grim Keepers

That night, a storm set in, bringing with it howling winds that swirled around and under my window hatches, causing an irritating vibration against the wall. I pulled my duvet up over my exposed shoulder, and shuddered at the cool evening air. My muscles clenched, fighting my stubbornness, demanding I get up and turn on the heat. Through gritted teeth, I grabbed my robe and draped it over my tired frame, inching my way downstairs. As I stepped into the kitchen I allowed my eyes to fully adjust to the darkness, waking me enough so I knew I would have trouble falling back to sleep.

I looked towards the swirling, battering sounds the storm played on my window, and gasped at what I saw. An old man stood at my window, raindrops hugging his now completely saturated face. His eyes opened unnaturally wide and I watched ants crawl out of his eye sockets in a terrifying march. My hands grasped the counter and I felt my own eyes mimicking his. My breath quickened as I tried to make sense of what I saw. I grabbed at a dish cloth and yanked it to my mouth like a toddler seeking comfort in a rotten piece of material, and unknowingly pulled a disregarded kitchen knife off the counter, sending it to its final resting place.

The Grim Keepers

The knife stood vertical whilst pinning my foot to the floor. I gurgled a scream through fear and shock, and arched my body to cope with the pain. I reached down, frantically fondling the skin around the knife, wondering if I should just yank it out or stay pinned to the floor.

I heard the sound of my key turning in the lock. The metal key clanked as it hit the kitchen floor. My breath stilled; I was stiff with fear, watching as the doorknob slowly turned. The door pushed the old rusty key along the tiled floor, which jumped along the patterned tiles and sounded an intimidating warning.

The terror of what was coming into my home consumed me. I was pinned to the spot and gasping for breath. Each footstep brought with it a squelch, most likely mud from the sodden yard, yet as I watched blood seeping from my foot my mind reminded me that the squelch could be anything. I closed my eyes, too afraid to face the unwelcome visitor, and curled into my wounded foot in some kind of defensive stance.

The man reached down and lifted my chin to meet his face. I didn't resist his spindly finger and hoped my compliance would encourage him to leave me alone. My eyes watched the march of the ants. If it wasn't so horrifying it would have been beautiful. The ants didn't scurry as though they were afraid; they had purpose and rhythm, suggesting this man had been their home for many years.

He studied my eyes, fixated on the terror he saw resting below the hopeful exterior. "You wish to live?" he said curiously, as though surprised anyone could want that.

My chin chattered in his ice-cold fingers, while tears percolated as I acknowledged my impending fate.

"Why me?" I managed to say. "Why me?"

"You witnessed the dance of the butterflies on the thirty-first night of the thirty-first moon. Your fate has been decided, my dear."

My foot throbbed and I absorbed the pain, wanting to remember every feeling before it was taken from me. The man seemed so real, so *there*. If he was dead, why did he feel so present?

I knew I had more fight in me. Why was I suddenly succumbing to a fate such as death? I grabbed the knife, yanking it from the floor, and in one swift move plunged it into the man's skull. His anger spiked and he began to grow. With outstretched arms his form blurred and changed as the knife lost all traction and fell through him to the floor. I scurried away, fighting with bated breath to move, to get to somewhere safe. The entity swirled around me in fragmented patterns, similar to the march of the ants. I hobbled my way through the house and reached the front door. I burst through it with such haste that I tripped on the welcome mat, launching myself straight into the pillar on the front porch. The impact was sudden and hard, and I immediately blacked out.

When I woke, I dragged my fingers through my hair, expecting to find blood. Instead, I was only met with a soft pillow, which cradled my face comfortingly.

I sat up in bed with a frightened start, ripping the duvet off so I could inspect my foot. It was fine. Last night had been nothing but a dream.

For the next week I avoided Cherry Oak Road, and decided the extra ten minutes each way was a good investment in my life. It took time for me to accept my vision hadn't been real, and I found myself jumping at the slightest surprise. My on-off boyfriend Malcolm agreed to come over for a few nights. He was a great distraction and found something endearing about my softened character. We grew closer that week and I was excited that our relationship finally seemed to move forward.

"You've changed, Jenny. You made it so hard for me to get close to you before, and I'd started to lose hope. You were always just so damn stubborn."

I chuckled at Malcolm's analysis. "I hadn't realized. I was just…well…you know. I was used to being on my own. For what it's worth, I'm glad I figured out why you backed off all the time. You could have just told me."

Malcolm laughed. "The old Jenny didn't want to hear it. Look, I've had a really great week with you. I think we have something here. I want to spend more time with you, see where things go. Is that okay?"

My grin spread wide across my blushing cheeks. Who knew a nightmare about death could make me feel so alive and in love?

I forced myself out of bed; lying next to Malcolm's warm body was heaven, but I wanted to make him a nice breakfast. I put some music on in the kitchen and searched for the flour and eggs. Pancakes with fresh strawberries and sweet cinnamon yogurt with a side of eggs. This was going to be good. I switched on the mini radio and played the 80's classics channel. The music always got me in the mood for cooking, and rather than a quick rinse and chop, the strawberries got serenaded in a loving bath, and I cleaned each berry to the beat.

The Grim Keepers

I reached across the counter and grabbed a kitchen knife from its holder, waving it through the air as I shimmied across the floor. My strawberry was perfectly positioned and as I went in for the kill, I froze.

The very tip of the blade was slightly bent, and a red mark stained the point. My mind raced, searching my memories to confirm my instant conclusion. This was the knife from my dream. I threw the blade down onto the chopping board and walked away. As I splashed cool water onto my face from the downstairs closet, I convinced myself I was being stupid and seeing things. With newfound confidence and a harsh reality check on myself, I went back into the kitchen to finish what I had started.

Malcolm stood at the chopping board with his back to me.

"Hey baby, you're awake. I didn't even hear you come down." I slid my arms around his naked torso. His body felt cold and ridged despite cozy, warm temperature of the kitchen.

"Malcolm, are you okay?" I took a tentative step backwards to allow him space to turn around. He didn't move, just continued to slice the strawberries, ignoring me completely. "Malcolm. Hey, hello? Earth to Malcolm." This time I stepped closer, but rather than nuzzle into his back I peered around him to look up at his face.

My eyes caught the mess before registering what it was. Blood pooled over the worktop as Malcolm sliced the fingers off his left hand. He had cut chunks off each one without a single sound.

I felt the terror tremble through me, rumbling like an unexpected storm. Vomit hit the floor before I even realized I was throwing up. The smell and taste of it brought another wave of rancid nausea. I stood helplessly over the sink as my body betrayed me multiple times.

Glancing up, I saw that same strange, familiar face just outside my window. An awkward smile now replaced his vacant stare. I felt myself lose control as my body fell to the floor and I fainted again.

My head pounded. I darted up and found myself in bed next to Malcolm, who slept soundly with all fingers intact. I couldn't fathom how a nightmare could be so realistic. It had taken me ages to get over the last one and now I felt that terror burrow into my heart once again.

My hands shook and I felt glued to the bed. I knew it was probably silly, and no doubt

The Grim Keepers

Malcolm would laugh if I told him, but I was afraid. Not only did I fear another dream, but I was gradually starting to hate my house—my home.

I nearly leaped out of bed when Malcolm reached over and placed an arm on my thigh. His cold touch shocked me. I burst into tears and cried for what felt like forever as Malcolm tried to calm me. Through each sob I managed to stutter one word, 'nightmare', making Malcolm's concern turn to amusement. His affection relaxed with him. He just didn't understand. I'd had nightmares as an early teen and remembered how they felt. This was something so different, so much more terrifying.

I called in sick for work, despite not wanting to be in the house at all. Malcolm refused to stay home on account of a bad dream, so I got ready and left with him, opting for the sanctuary of my favorite coffee shop in town.

It was now over a week past Halloween, yet decorations dominated every yard and the cafe still had little hand-decorated pumpkin cookies and cut out lanterns, which delighted the kids. It was quiet today and I sat alone, sipping my Cappuccino while captivated by 'The Concierge', a new novel I had just started. The story had me totally gripped; my eyes barely left the page until I noticed someone sitting on the other side of the room. The figure had his back to me, but I hadn't see him enter the coffee shop. *Surely I would have noticed someone walking past the table*, I thought. Regardless, I continued to read, sucked into the imaginary drama that made me forget about my own.

I always hated getting to that last dreg of coffee. It posed a difficult question of whether or not to order another. I knew I shouldn't, but going home was not an option. I approached the checkout but couldn't see Louise. Instead, I saw the stranger shuffle to my left, and as I leaned forward to try to see through the back door, I felt his presence right behind me. I turned and smiled to politely say, 'Get off my ass,' but was met with a ghastly face—that face, his face, covered in ants.

My eyes popped in shock and doubt. I cautiously looked around me, refusing to accept the vision for what it was—refusing to allow myself to register it as nothing more than the sick things my mind had conjured up.

The man reached his hand out and gripped my neck, forcing me back against the counter. He pushed me further until I caught a glimpse of Louise, pale and lifeless, crumpled behind the counter. I felt the anger surge inside me, filling my arms with sudden strength to push this thing's hands off me. In one swift move I was free, out the door and running down the street. It was broad daylight. *How the hell is this happening to me? Am I losing my mind?*

I found myself backing into a kids' park, looking around continuously like a crazy fool. Two moms exchanged puzzled glances, seeing the terror I carried like a heavy rucksack.

"Are you okay?" the dark haired lady asked, walking up to me and placing a reassuring hand on my arm.

"No. Yes…no…I don't know. Honestly, I don't know. I'm afraid." I looked the woman dead in the eyes, amazed at the frantic words that just spewed out of my mouth. If I were her, I know what I would be thinking, but she looked so kind with soft, forgiving eyes. They were eyes that had dealt with a crazy toddler for so long that nothing was surprising.

"Do you want me to call someone for you?"

"Yes. Malcolm. Call Malcolm to come and get me please." I handed over my cell phone that looked like it was stuck on vibrate while wedged between my fingers. It had dents where I had gripped it so hard, unable to actually use the damn thing.

I didn't enjoy sitting in the park waiting for Malcolm to arrive. The kind moms let their kids run around me and ask me funny questions. They probably thought I was harmless and that it would be a good distraction, but I worried for them. I felt an evil within me, swirling inside, toying with my visions. Whatever was happening to me, I didn't want anyone else to get hurt. Louise at the coffee shop had only been eighteen.

When Malcolm arrived he took me straight to the car, thanking the women who called him.

"I can see how visibly shaken up you are. What happened?"

"I had more visions. But this time, Malcolm, I'm still awake. Look at me. There's no way this can be a dream. The man with the ants was in the coffee shop and I think he killed Louise!"

Malcolm looked at me with compassionate doubt. I saw the confusion battling within him. "Should we go back to the coffee shop and check on Louise?"

"You don't believe me?"

"Sure I do. If what you say actually happened, we have to call someone."

The Grim Keepers

The thought of going back there seemed worse than going home, but Malcolm was right; we had to go.

I couldn't believe my eyes when we got there. The cafe was busy, Louise serving customers with that same welcoming smile I had come to expect. She looked at me with puzzled bemusement, like she wanted to remind me that I knew her. I just couldn't believe she was okay. An hour earlier she was dead; I had seen her body. I felt then like my own was crossing over between worlds. I felt things that seemed real but couldn't possibly be.

We drove home in silence. I was now convinced something was wrong and Malcolm was now convinced I was crazy.

That night, my behavior was completely erratic. I paced around the house and rearranged things, trying to seek comfort in a familiar setting. Malcolm only watched me, and I knew he was thinking hard—probably searching for the best moment to leave and never come back.

He picked up the landline and went to the bathroom. When he returned he looked remarkably sad.

"Are you okay?" I asked. He looked so pale I wondered if he had seen him—the man.

The Grim Keepers

"I'm okay. I was just chatting with your mom. She and I agree…"

"My mom? What are you talking about? My mom's dead. Is that meant to be funny, or some kind of trick to test how crazy I really am?"

Malcolm looked down at his feet and sighed. He looked helpless, like he had given up.

The people that came to my house looked friendly enough. They said sweet things to coax me into a protective jacket to keep everyone safe. I fought and screamed and kicked with every ounce of strength I had, but I knew no one believed me. They had decided I was lost already.

I swear I saw tears in Malcolm's eyes as they dragged me through the door. When I looked back at my home from the sidewalk before being bundled into the ambulance, I saw my delicate wooden house overcome with evil, like a morning haze across a grassy field. Malcolm wasn't safe there either, and I saw him, the man from my dreams, standing in the kitchen window. This time he was smiling.

I felt incredible, agonizing panic as the drivers took me away. I no longer believed there was a place of safety and sanity for me. This nightmare owned me and would be with me forever.

The Grim Keepers

The ambulance didn't turn right at the end of the street toward the hospital, but instead took a left, heading toward a dead-end known as Cherry Oak Road. The stagnant street that warned of death had taken me, another victim, of the thirty-first night on the thirty-first moon.

As the ambulance drove down the pretty, tree-lined street, I wondered if things would be different had I just spared those extra ten minutes every day.

The ambulance faded from view after delivering me to my fate, the house that stood closest to the road. My disappearance would soon be told as nothing more than an age-old tale of Cherry Oak Road.

About Laura Callender

As the founder of CWC (Collaborative Writing Challenge), and the newly launched publishing company: CW Publishing House, Laura has mainly focused on developing her concept to bring writers together to produce full-length fiction novels. She gets very little time to write at the moment, but couldn't resist contributing to this fun anthology. Laura has published one children's book and has two more on the way. You can

The Grim Keepers

connect with Laura using the following links:

LinkedIn: www.linkedin.com/in/lauracallender
Twitter: @CollaborativeWC
Website:
www.collaborativewritingchallenge.com

Facebook:
www.facebook.com/Collaborativewritingchalleng
e

The Grim Keepers

Crafted With Daddy
By Cayce Berryman

Mara couldn't refuse the endless pools of green glistening at her, pleading for another chance. The endless things lost to those eyes had emptied her shed of most of her supplies, and now her daughter wanted to use something else. She tried to hide a smile but gave in when her smart little girl caught the twitch and beamed.

"Thank you," she squealed happily as she bolted out the door with a rope dangling between her tiny legs, trailing from the wadded mess she clutched in her hand. Mara's nerves rumbled steadily inside her as she wondered what an eight-year-old wanted markers and a rope for, though Kristy *had* been inventive lately. While most children her age drew half-decent drawings of their parents, Kristy had found a way to make a dog-like figure out of sticks, glue, and rubber bands. Her detail impressed Mara, each shade of brown placed intuitively in a proper place until the shades blended into a uniform brown mutt shaded by the sun. It was nice to see Kristy interested in something, even if she rarely saw the result of her disappearing supplies. She always received the same excuse when Kristy didn't return with whatever she had taken with her. "It's part of the woods now," she'd say.

"Be careful, sweetie," she called out as Kristy scampered across the small field and into the woods. Mara always watched the bright-colored shirt dwindle amongst the trees, making sure Kristy followed the rules and didn't pass the line Mara had made for her a year prior. Mara had tried to sneak out there a few times to see the things she had made, but they were never there. It worried her that Kristy might be walking deeper into the woods than she was allowed, but after a few days of watching out for her highlighter-colored shirts, Mara assumed animals had taken them or torn them up.

Kristy loved the woods, though it had taken two years for her to go near them. It seemed

The Grim Keepers

weird to Mara that Kristy's previous phobia of the woods had turned into an almost intrinsic desire for its presence. Living so close to the woods, Mara eventually let the thought go, thankful for the change. Mara never asked Kristy how she felt about things or why, and tried not to bring it up. Last time she asked her little girl about why she did something, the emerald eyes rounded into frightened, questioning stares that gave Mara nightmares. "Why don't you want to talk to your dad?" she had asked, and now knew it to be a mistake.

When Kristy reacted the same way with every question regarding her emotions, Mara decided it best to avoid the topic altogether. It made her sick to see her little girl hide in her room for hours after questions like that, and it didn't make sense. For months, she nearly dragged Kristy to the cemetery to 'visit' her daddy, reminding her that his death wasn't empty like she said it was.

"It's empty, mommy. Death is empty."

Words like that hurt Mara. Michael's murder wasn't meaningless; it had saved their daughter. A previous debt of Michael's had brought the dangerous man into their world, but Michael didn't hesitate to protect his family.

The Grim Keepers

Michael's obsessions always brought danger to their house, and his previous obsession with porn created a rift in their relationship, almost ripping it apart when Michael tried recording others for his own pleasure. Dark times had veiled their household, but Michael had changed, and his previous obsessions disappeared when he caught a glimpse of their first sonogram.

After her birth, Michael obsessed over Kristy, refusing to leave her side from the moment they locked eyes. It had scared Mara a little in the beginning, but Kristy's bond with her father made the relationship so pure and wonderful, and Mara's initial nerves dissipated in the mesmerizing green eyes of her little girl.

As usual, Kristy trotted up the hill toward the house as the sun set behind her into the trees. The rope no longer dangled behind her, but the markers remained clutched in her fists. Mara squinted at a red mark across Kristy's neck and hoped the red marker had caused it.

"You're leaving with black next time," she grumbled as a shudder ran down her spine. She fought the urge to run to her, knowing Kristy would panic if she heard the fear in her mommy's voice. "What's on your neck, dear?" she asked simply as Kristy skipped into the doorway.

The Grim Keepers

The emerald eyes darted around to meet her own. They seemed flat, tired, and ready for a quick bath and bed. Dirt speckled around her eyes and coated her hands in a thin layer of brown that fell to the floor in soft clumps as she rubbed her hands against her tree-splintered jeans. "Hm?" she asked.

Mara shook her head and knelt beside her daughter, rubbing at the mark that sparked into urgency as it came away wet, revealing an open, raw-skinned burn. "What were you doing today?" she demanded, no longer concerned with hurting her daughter's feelings.

Kristy frowned and pushed herself away from Mara's grasp. "Playing," she defended herself, and crossed her arms over her chest.

She was trying to shut down, but Mara wouldn't let her. "This is a rash, Kristy. Or a burn. And it's not…" She sighed and grabbed her forehead. "Just…take a shower, please. I'll look at that when it's cleaned up."

Kristy ran into the restroom and slammed the door behind her. Mara wondered if her daughter could only feel extreme happiness or complete distress because of how quickly they interchanged with each other, but she dropped the thought and concerned herself with the cause of her daughter's rash. It could have been a rope burn, but Kristy would not have been strong enough to do anything that would cause a heavy burn like that. Her neck felt more than raw, almost fleshy, and the skin had broken enough to spread blood across the front of her neck toward her chin.

Water trickled to life from the shower and shut off a short ten minutes later. Kristy stepped out of the bathroom in her underwear and Mara motioned her over, calming herself this time before inspecting the wound. Her insides churned as Kristy thrust her head upward in a spiteful gesture. The burn barely changed, only lighter now that the dirt had washed away. She struggled to stay angry, knowing she shouldn't be letting an eight-year-old out of her sight anyway.

"Where's the rope?"

Kristy shrugged, and Mara asked again, this time growing impatient.

"You better find it and bring it home tomorrow."

Kristy's face changed, her little attitude gone. "But, it's—"

"Don't care."

"It's for daddy!" she screamed.

Tears slid down her cheek, and Mara's heart sank. Kristy's mention of her dad made the burn a fading scar in Mara's eyes, and she tried to control the tears threatening to flood down her heated cheeks. "What?"

Kristy glared through glassy eyes and bolted into her room. She slammed the door, and Mara knew she'd hide in there for hours, so she would be asleep by the time she ever considered emerging.

Mara walked to the back porch and gazed into the darkening shadows of the woods. Now, she found herself curious in the project Kristy had started. Kristy had crafted many things, refusing to show her mom because she claimed they would wake up and live with the other animals in the woods, but this time she felt she needed to know, especially if it was meant for Michael.

A light danced around the branches and disappeared, appearing again like a large firefly making a presence in the trees. Squinting, Mara decided she would overlook the burn, reminding herself Kristy was bound to get hurt eventually. She sighed, shut the door, and walked into her bedroom for the night.

***

Curiosity drove Mara's thoughts around the room as she tried to consider the things her daughter had been creating, and if Michael was the inspiration for the secrets in the woods. Kristy hadn't even made an appearance, and she wondered if she was still upset. Figuring out how her daughter's emotions worked now seemed a futile thing since the strange change occurred a week after Michael died. Even five months later, Kristy's interests only lay in the woods and the projects in which she engulfed herself. How could Mara say no? She knew she'd have to do something eventually but had decided to wait until she could at least contain her own emotions. At this point, the only thing she managed to control were the tears fighting to break the brims of her eyes at every moment, especially when she saw the glorious velvet-green eyes that glanced at her with the same sincerity Michael's had.

"Kristy?" she called out, and turned her head when she didn't receive a response. "Kristy. Come here." Mara moved from her room, knowing she would probably be waking a sleeping rock, and walked to Kristy's door, knocking firmly for an answer. "What's the rule? I will let you have your private space if you answer when I call you."

Frustrated, Mara broke the promise she made to Kristy a week after Michael's death and opened the door. Kristy's moods were hard to decipher in the beginning, and they had agreed to give her 'private space' so she could be alone when she wanted to. At first it seemed like a good idea, and Mara hoped the space would help Kristy share more with her mom when she was ready. Now, it was starting to become ridiculous, and Mara felt the urge to be a 'friend' during their mourning ebb.

The empty room intensified the frustration exploding in her chest as anger replaced the constant despair she'd felt for months. Among the many simple rules, Kristy's ultimate rule was to never leave without telling her mom. For months, Kristy had traveled in and out of the woods, building or creating things out of trash and plastic, tape and rubber bands. The routine had strict protocol determined by Mara, and for the first time it had been broken.

She bolted out the back door, eyeing the trees for a flash of bright clothing. Her eyes darted above and around her as she entered the woods, scanning its depths for a sign of her daughter. The moon barely lit the ground below the trees, so she stared into the black areas of the woods for a while and listened. Her heartbeat roared in her ears, and she sprinted along the edge of the woods where she had seen Kristy before from the kitchen window.

"Kristy!" she screamed.

Kristy didn't answer, but Mara heard the rustle of feet escaping into the yard behind their house. She ran after the sound and sped up with fury igniting beneath her feet as she caught the familiar scurry in Kristy's legs. She easily caught up with her and spun her around to scream fear into her daughter.

Mara dropped her arms and fell back onto her backside. The silver sheen that glittered in Kristy's eyes glared down at her in the remaining moonlight. Her hands dripped with a dark liquid, and the same liquid darkened the skin on her neck and streaked down her chest. Kristy smiled, her eyes wide and joyful like an entrancing game she couldn't escape.

A soft wind encircled them, and Mara searched for words, trying to remember the anger that had driven her forward moments ago. "Kristy," was all she could whisper into the chilled air, the words like ice on her tongue. Kristy didn't acknowledge the name, but only turned toward the house to run as she just had moments before. Mara shoved herself forward to follow, but a tight pull on her heart kept her in place. Another breeze blew, and she turned toward the woods, hoping her real daughter would emerge. A soft, inaudible whisper pleaded with a strangely familiar voice, almost beckoning, and she stepped toward it with a curiosity she had never felt before. Her heart thudded as the whispers grew louder, more familiar, and a sudden scream from her daughter's bedroom shook her from the trance and sent her sprinting toward the house.

"Kristy!" Mara screamed, racing through her daughter's doorway without any consideration of the previous vision. Kristy lay on her floor, covered in wet sheets that wrapped around her neck and waist. She kicked and swung her thin arms around her, eyes horror-stricken and desperate. Mara knelt beside her and curled the mass of sweat and cloth into her chest as she called her name in an attempt to wake her. Kristy wept, and Mara looked at her face for the foreign eyes she had seen, but only scared, emerald gems reflected light through the tears spilling from her eyes.

"Mom," she mumbled through shattered gasps. "Mom."

"I'm here, baby. Just a dream." Mara wiped hot tears from the sides of her cheeks and stared intently at the beautiful, green eyes. She couldn't question what she saw, but nothing could explain it either. Whatever Kristy had seen was all that mattered now, and the strange whispers that now only drifted like wind into the house didn't let rest the chill driving into Mara's thoughts. She breathed in her own tears and shuddering cries, hoping to comfort her daughter from the living nightmare they had just experienced.

Shaking the memory of the silver eyes that had overtaken Kristy made sleeping difficult, and the voice she heard only resonated through her ears as fresh as a present memory, shifting with the eyes in her dreams as they scanned Mara's face with desire and an empty truth. She woke several times throughout the night, peeking through the crack she'd left in Kristy's doorway to make sure she still lay in bed asleep. "No more woods," she decided, and closed the door to her daughter's room.

***

Panic threw Mara's eyes open, the knowledge that she had fallen asleep this time like an alarm demanding her attention. She ran into Kristy's room and her daughter sat upright in her bed, her eyes full of new betrayal.

"Mom!"

"Sorry," Mara said and shut the door as

relief washed over her. She'd broken her boundary, but that was okay. Kristy didn't seem afraid now, and her flashing green eyes looked normal.

Shaking her head, Mara decided her panic last night may have exaggerated what she saw, though the memory of the silver eyes didn't go away. Walking into the kitchen to make breakfast, she knew Kristy would have another day planned for the woods, but she couldn't push the nerves that twisted in her at the thought. Whether her mind had distorted things last night didn't dissolve the fear that now filled her from the mass of trees and dark, invisible life. She didn't remember seeing Kristy's project either, though it, too, could have been hidden in the shadows behind the moon's revealing light.

"Bye!" Kristy smiled as she stuffed a piece of toast in her mouth.

Mara's daze barely broke in time for her to swing around, snatching Kristy's arm with a firm squeeze. "No," she warned.

Kristy reeled to meet her gaze, dumbstruck. "I ate toast. It's breakfast."

"You went out there without telling me, and you went at night. That's two strikes, Kristy."

"No I didn't!"

"Three strikes for lying. No more woods."

"What?"

Mara's heart ripped at the sight of her daughter's heartbroken gaze. "I won't play games with you."

"I didn't lie. I wasn't in the woods."

Mara laughed airily, disbelief plain on her face. "Do you not remember me catching you last night? That's enough. I'll go get your projects for you, but you're not allowed out there. Where are they?"

"Nowhere!" she screamed through furious tears. "They belong to the woods."

The words tugged a nerve. Mara didn't care to hear that anymore. "If you don't tell me, how will you finish your project for daddy?" she decided to say, sure Kristy had left to work on it. Really though, the fact that Kristy refused to tell her where they were made Mara more curious about what she had done with her projects.

"I can only finish it in the woods."

"Well you're not going to the woods. You should have thought about that when you snuck out."

"I didn't sneak out." The words were a hiss and tears followed down her face. Kristy whipped around and stormed into her bedroom, slamming the door behind her and twisting the lock in place.

Mara considered busting the door down, frustration testing her mood. Kristy's rule-breaking would drive them both to insanity. She couldn't allow her daughter to have a 'privacy room' if she wanted to force her mother out. She sighed and faced the line of trees she had just forbidden her child to enter. Guilt flooded her, reminding her that she had removed the only thing Kristy wanted to do and the only apparent connection she somehow related to her father. Tears welled, and she tried to shove away the memory that now slammed against the front of her thoughts.

She wished she had been more concerned with who had knocked on the door, but she never thought the man who burst in would demand to see Michael or threaten his family. The gun had flashed about the room like a glistening gem, a dangerous weapon aimed to collect a payment of suffering.

***

"What does he owe?" Mara had asked, pressing herself against the back door in case Kristy came running home with Michael. She didn't like the woods, but she would eagerly wait outside the mass of thick trees and brush for her dad while he searched for the mushrooms she loved. "What did he do?"

The man threw the gun up, and she looked down the undesirable depths of the cold, lifeless barrel. "What did he do? Damn husband was watching me and my wife."

"What?" she gasped, her heart dropping into her stomach with a hard slam. "No, he's been home… Here. He stopped—"

"Yeah, I'm sure. Thought so too, until I caught him again the other day. First time I've caught him in years."

"But…" She almost asked how he was sure it was her husband but stopped short. "I'm really sorry." She tried to steady her breath, wondering if she would pay the price for what now seemed a long-forgotten past.

"*He* will be." The man's eyes flickered with a new light, and Mara followed his gaze to the little girl running from the woods toward the door. Michael followed behind, his care-free grin seeming to drown the idea of his former demons come to haunt him again.

Mara glanced at the man and breathed deeply before shoving into him. He grabbed her arm, swinging her into a bar stool that fell against the door. Mara tried pulling herself off the ground, but he lifted her onto her feet again and dragged her away, throwing her to the ground in the living room and stomping out the back door. A scream and a desperate cry sent Mara tumbling forward toward the door, her vision throwing things sporadically out of place. She fumbled for the knob and threw it open, the knot catching in her chest as her daughter struggled against the man's grip on her with the gun to her head.

"No!" she screamed, her mind running wild as she ran toward the man. He swung Kristy around and pressed the gun to her head in warning. Mara stopped.

She eyed Michael, whose hands reached forward in hopes of earning their child back. "I swear, it wasn't me watching you."

"You're the only bastard I've ever caught watching me. Hell with you!"

"I haven't... I couldn't be more sorry for what I did in the past, but I swear it wasn't me. I have a daughter. I have..." He choked, his arms trembling toward his daughter.

The man cocked his head until his neck popped. "If it happens again, it'll be on video. For now, hopefully she'll teach you something."

Mara ran toward the man, but Michael beat

her to him. He jerked Kristy out of his grasp as a shot rang through the air. Mara fell to the ground and pulled her daughter in her arms, and another shot stole sound from the once beautiful day. Another shot, and Mara buried Kristy's face into her shoulder, hiding her own face in her daughter's hair as the sound of a falling body hit the grass.

***

"Stop!" Mara screamed, pressing her hands over her ears. She fell to her knees beside the counter, crying into the memory through restrained pleas for her husband. "Stop."

The words seemed to drown the vivid memory away, and Mara caught her breath in time to see Kristy peek through a crack in her doorway. She sighed, knowing her daughter had heard the same words she had once used, but Kristy closed the door and left Mara to pick herself up.

Kristy didn't argue when Mara told her to meet her in the 'Schoolroom', an office space next to Kristy's bedroom they used for her homeschooling. The lesson went quick, and Kristy hid in her room again after the lesson ended. Mara didn't argue and looked out into the woods again, knowing she still needed to search for the project Kristy had worked on. Curiosity tugged, and she decided she'd leave after dinner so Kristy wouldn't have a reason to come out of her room and find her mother gone.

***

The sun kissed the tops of the trees as she walked into its shadowed world. She planned on leaving before the sun set, but it was surprisingly difficult to tell the time of day from beneath the branches. The forest was thick, lush, and beautiful, and Mara wondered why she had never entered the woods herself. She felt peace and the uneasiness of walking into the woods dissipated as she searched for sign of anything that didn't belong there.

Darkness enveloped the woods almost too soon. It hadn't seemed like a lot of time had passed, but when Mara found a break in the trees above her, the moon shone bright at its peak in the sky. She didn't know how she had managed to stay in the woods as long as she did, and she hadn't found sign of any of Kristy's projects. She had even walked a little deeper in case Kristy had snuck out before to hide her projects. With an irritated sigh, Mara glanced at the moon once more as it disappeared above the trees and continued to walk toward home.

A soft whisper stopped her, and she turned

toward the darkness in the trees as she had the night before. The voice sounded more clear now, louder and familiar. She listened and tried to pick out the words, but a rustling sound broke her from falling into a trance and she jerked around. Kristy walked past her like she didn't exist. Mara's anger boiled and she reached to pull her daughter backward, but she instead watched her go.

Kristy continued to walk without a thought to stop her, so Mara followed, curiosity in her direction pulling her forward but preventing her interception. Kristy had broken the rules yet again, but something strange had seemed to take over her daughter's awkwardly stiff steps, her body now a straight pillar of determined thought. Mara shook the chill curling her body into a cold torrent of fear and hoped Kristy was sleepwalking. She knew better, but she needed some kind of comfort to continue following her daughter, who didn't seem to care otherwise.

The whispering continued. It grew louder, but the words weren't any more clear. Kristy answered them with whispers of her own, giggling softly as if she were having a conversation with a friend. Mara shook her head and struggled to hear the words, but the sound of them froze her in place as Kristy turned around to face her, the silver glow in her eyes as present and real as the night before.

"Daddy," she whispered, facing a tree that separated Mara from her daughter. Kristy looked up, so Mara followed her gaze to a dark shadow that lay high above the trees. A rope dangled from a branch, and Kristy jumped toward it, barely catching it in her fingers as it pulled down with her.

Mara screamed, the large silhouette breaking apart while things hit the ground and blew dirt in every direction. The moon lit the ground, brightly revealed in the open space above the trees, and Mara backed away with disbelieving eyes. She looked at Kristy, but her daughter didn't seem to notice her as she rummaged through the junk. She came out of the mess with a jar of black liquid and proceeded to spread it across her neck as she spoke softly to the whispering voice.

"For you, daddy," she said.

She started to walk forward, scared for what her daughter wanted to do, but the whispering voice answered back with words Mara recognized. "Death is empty, Kristy."

Mara walked toward the mess and recognized the materials Kristy had used in the previous months. Nothing seemed put together, but Kristy stared at it with pride behind her silver eyes. Mara opened her mouth to speak but jumped back as Kristy lifted her little arms into the air, her fingers oozing with the black liquid. The junk shook and pieces lifted into the air with an invisible hand to control them.

"Kirs—" Mara tried to say, but something held her throat closed and she fell into the ground, scratching at her neck for air. She opened her mouth to scream, but nothing came out.

"Death is empty," the voice said again, and she felt a presence beside her that she couldn't see. It held her, removing all air from her lungs and holding her from reaching for her daughter. Kristy climbed on a box she had used, one of the first things she'd taken from the garage. Pieces of wood had been nailed into the trees, and Kristy climbed on them and grabbed a metal ratchet lodged into the bark beside a large branch.

Mara sucked in air, gasping as her vision distorted itself and a tingling feeling spread all over her body. She screamed for Kristy, but her silent voice echoed in her ears as if a wall kept the voice inside. The tingling spread into her stomach and legs, and she thrashed about to find its source. She rose to her feet and tried stumbling toward Kristy, but her legs gave from under her and she slipped into the dirt again.

Kristy crawled along the branch, and the rope she had taken most recently dangled lightly over it. Kristy pulled it up and her eyes drifted across the ground until their silver pupils found Mara, helpless on the ground.

She smiled. "Death is empty, mommy." The words echoed like tormenting strikes in a memory, and Mara screamed again as she pulled herself up without thinking.

"Kristy!" she cried, but her daughter didn't seem to hear her. She walked toward her, her body moving without conscious intention. "Kristy, what's wrong?" Her words didn't seem to penetrate her daughter's entranced mind, and the smile created a foreign look that Mara didn't recognize. "What's happening!"

"Daddy misses us," she whispered, and Mara stood beneath the branch from which Kristy looked down at her. Mara shook her head, though a calm had washed over the panic she felt she should have felt.

"What's wrong, Kristy?" she pleaded, wishing she had grabbed her daughter when she first saw her.

Kristy looked deeper into the woods and giggled. "We belong to the woods now."

The Grim Keepers

"No, Kristy."

"Daddy told me what to do. He says me first."

The rope fell from the branches and tumbled down until it stopped in front of Mara. She stopped breathing, the bright red noose tight around the wooden dog she had made. The dog fell out as the noose widened, and Mara tried shoving herself away from the rope. Something held her though, and the noose rose into the trees again. Kristy wrapped it around her neck, smiling as she glanced down at the dog that had held firm in its decent.

"Kristy!" Mara screamed, unable to move. "Kristy, wake up. This isn't real. Daddy isn't here. Please, Kristy!"

Her daughter giggled as she leapt from the trees. The rope lessened in slack as Mara watched, horror-stricken, until the rope tightened and a small, dangling body jerked around. The invisible hold on her broke, and Mara screeched inaudibly as she ran to her daughter's side. Fear enveloped the girl's eyes, the silver now the innocent, emerald green darkened with terror. Mara pulled her daughter into her arms and tugged at the knot around her neck, but the rope wouldn't loosen. Screaming, she struggled with Kristy as they both fumbled for the rope, but Kristy stopped and her body stiffened.

"Kristy!" she cried, screaming as the body went limp in her arms. The presence surrounded her and chilled her bones, but she ignored it as she managed to loosen the knot, not noticing as it loosened into a wider, larger loop.

She cried, washing her hands over her daughter's face and burying her sobs into Kristy's neck. She felt the presence tightening on her muscles, and she jerked upward before it could control her.

"Death is empty," the voice said, and Mara struggled to fight the presence entering her head.

"No," she growled through battered tears. She tried to process or understand what happened, but the recognizable presence ended her questioning and stopped her in place as she looked out into the field behind her house. She turned on her heels, smiling slightly as the voice enveloped her thoughts.

"Michael."

Something in her cried for freedom, but Michael's presence forced new thoughts in her head, and she couldn't stop their driving force. "Come home."

She nodded and walked back toward the

noose, setting her daughter on the ground before walking up the makeshift steps and grabbing the jar of black liquid. She grinned into the silver eyes that shone back at her in its reflection and an image of the man who killed Michael flashed in its black depths, the next one to be drawn deep in the woods. She smiled again and wrapped the noose around her neck. "Death is empty."

About Cayce Berryman

Cayce Berryman claims her freelance editing and her own writing as her passions above all else. However, she humbles herself with the knowledge that all writers and editors can always learn more. She offers a variety of editing services, both for fiction and non-fiction works. She also owns and runs an interactive Facebook group, "An Author's Tale," which serves as a building platform for budding writers and published authors. The Lord fuels her faith daily, and she makes sure to include Him in all she does.

Contact or connect with Cayce:
Website/Blog: www.cayceberryman.com
Facebook:
https://www.facebook.com/pages/Cayce-

The Grim Keepers

Berryman-Writer/1546794008925725
An Author's Tale:
https://www.facebook.com/groups/anauthorstale

The Grim Keepers

Crepuscular
by Rachel Fox

"It's for the best, Mrs. Watson, believe me. We can look after her, keep her safe."

Sophie sat on the edge of the bed, her feet hanging just above the floor. Her long black hair fanned out across her bare knees. She heard her mother's sobs but didn't respond. The drugs had made her sluggish, and she was enjoying it.

"You can call any time, day or night, and visit whenever you like." The nurse was talking again. "We have no restrictions, but call first in case it's a...difficult time."

There was more talking, but Sophie had dissolved into her thoughts so she didn't hear what was said. She was vaguely aware of her mother touching her shoulder, maybe kissing her on the head, and then it was dark. She stared up at the ceiling as it bled in and out of focus above her. Darkness on darkness. Shadows on shadows. She couldn't differentiate her body from the bed, couldn't tell if she was flesh and blood or metal and fabric. She didn't care.

She hadn't always felt this way, couldn't remember when it started. Maybe it was when her dad left, or when her mum married Jeff. Maybe it was when the disgusting sprog arrived, and she had been moved to the box room like an unwanted piece of furniture. Maybe it was the way the other girls excluded her at school, or when Mark dumped her. Maybe it was just normal teenage stuff. All she knew was that on that day, at that moment, she hadn't wanted to live another second, let alone another day. All she'd wanted, needed, was relief from the crushing pain inside her.

She ran her nails over the bandages at her wrist, evidence of her failure. They thought it was a cry for help because she'd done such a terrible job of it, but it wasn't. She'd barely scratched the surface before her mother found her. She sat up and began to wrestle the bandages free. They fell slack onto the bed and she examined the crusted welts. Crying silently, she pulled at the scabs. The pain echoed up her arm, dampening the pain in her heart. She breathed out heavily as the tiny scarlet beads bloomed on her skin as she rested back on the bed.

She heard it before she saw it—a faint, pitiful mewling. She thought she had imagined it but the room was dark and quiet, and when it came again, she was sure it was real. She sat up, resting herself on her elbow, and squinted into the dark corner. The sound came again and the shadows shifted. She held her breath and watched. At first it seemed to have no form, being nothing but a small blob of blackness crawling across the floor towards her. It moved slowly and painfully, pulsing as it made its way into the middle of the room. Moonlight ripped a tear across the floor, and as the creature moved into it, she could see it was a kitten. Tiny and barely formed, its eyes were closed and its black fur matted to its skin. It limped further towards her, but she was off the bed by then, leaping towards it. It flinched as she landed on floor next to it.

She picked the animal up gently, feeling its fragile frame in her hands, knowing she could crush it if she wanted to. She carried it to the bed and cradled it to her chest, whispering "It's okay, you're safe now."

The kitten nuzzled into her palm, stretching its head towards her as if reaching for something "What are you after?" she asked.

It wriggled in her hands, mewling even more desperately. She loosened her grip and it sprang forward. Sophie felt its rough tongue, dry and ragged, brush against her wrist. The kitten moved its head from side to side, purring as it settled against her skin, and licked at the beads of drying blood.

"Are you hungry?" she asked.

It sucked and chewed on her flesh, lapping and pulling at the slash on her wrist. She rested back on the bed, enjoying in equal measure the pain and the warmth of the kitten's body. She didn't want to think anymore so she closed her eyes and slept.

Daylight woke her. She looked around for the kitten, but there was no sign of it despite the fact that there was no way in or out of the room. The wound was red and angry and the bandages lay in a heap on the floor. She wondered if she had dreamt it, but she wasn't sure. Hearing voices outside her room, she quickly wrapped the bandages back around her arm as best she could and pretended to be asleep.

The Grim Keepers

"Wake up, Sophie," the nurse said gently/ Sophie liked her voice. "Wake up now, it's lunch time." Sophie yawned and pretended to stretch, turning to face the nurse who sat on the end of her bed. She was in her forties, Sophie guessed, around the same age as her mother though it was difficult to judge; her hands looked older, her eyes younger. She offered Sophie a sandwich but she refused it.

"You must eat something, Sophie, for me."

Her smile was warm and kind, so Sophie let her feed her a spoonful or two of ice cream. She enjoyed being babied though she would never admit it. The nurse said her name was Nurse Barton and that she was there to help. Sophie believed her.

They talked while Sophie took her tablets and Nurse Barton changed her dressings. She was nice. She was calm, unlike her mother, who always seemed to be in the middle of some kind of drama or other. Sophie liked her.

"Do you want to take a walk to the television room today, Sophie?" Nurse Barton asked, but Sophie shook her head and shimmied back under the covers. She wasn't ready for that.

"That's okay. Maybe tomorrow," Nurse Barton said. Sophie heard her leave the room before the drugs took hold.

When she woke up it was dusk. The shadows heaved as they had the night before, and Sophie peered into the blackness.

"Are you here, little kitten?"

She heard it purr as it crawled towards her. She felt the weight of it land on her stomach. This was not a dream; this was real. The kitten moved quickly to her wrist and nuzzled at the blankets. Sophie knew what it wanted. She wanted it too. She pulled her leaden arm from under the blanket and pushed the bandages out of the way. She jumped when the kitten bit at her flesh, its sharp needle teeth undoing the healing wound and sucking deeply on her blood. She relaxed then, let her eyes roll back and let the pain flood through her body, cleansing her, releasing her.

She was vaguely aware of the kitten leaving this time. It seemed bigger, more tangible than it had when it first crawled out from the shadows. She pulled the bandages back over her wrist and rolled towards the wall. When she next opened her eyes it was very light in the room. Sunlight streamed through the window and stung her eyes.

"You've been asleep for a long time, Sophie. The doctor came to see you, but you slept right through his visit!" It was Nurse Barton. Sophie managed a smile.

"You have a nice smile." Nurse Barton sounded pleased. "I like to see you smile, Sophie."

Nurse Barton chatted gently to her as she arranged a table next to the bed and rested a tray with a sandwich and a drink on it.

"It's cheese. Everyone likes cheese, don't they?" Nurse Barton said cheerfully, helping Sophie to sit up.

"Do you like cats?" Sophie asked.

"I'm more of a dog person, to be honest," Nurse Barton said, plumping the bed pillows. "Do you?"

"Yes," Sophie said, glancing towards the corner but knowing it would be empty.

"That's nice," "Nurse Barton said.

"Do you ever have cats here at the hospital?"

Nurse Barton laughed. "No animals here, honey. It wouldn't be allowed. Silly rule, really. Now try and eat something, I'll be back in to check on you before I go home."

Sophie took a bite of the sandwich and chewed on it two or three times before giving up and spitting it out. She wasn't hungry. She squashed half of the sandwich under her mattress,

115

saving it for the kitten, and left the rest on the plate. Nurse Barton returned an hour or so later and told her she'd done well. Sophie felt a pang of guilt for lying, but it passed soon enough. She swallowed her tablets with some of the drink and let Nurse Barton change the bandages on her wrist.

"This isn't healing as well as I'd like," she said as she smeared on some sour-smelling cream and wound the bandage up a little more tightly than before.

Sophie was glad to sink back into sleep, and again when she woke it was dark. The kitten was on her chest, its tail towards her, flicking in her face. The pain radiated up her arm. The sweetness of it relaxed her, and she didn't try to move until the kitten had finished. It shifted off her chest and jumped onto the floor. She lifted her head to see it. It was big, twice the size it had been two nights ago. It was now a fully grown cat, sleek and muscular.

"Cat," she said. It was all she could manage. It turned to look at her, but she couldn't see its eyes. They were as black as its fur, as black as the shadow into which it disappeared.

Nurse Barton came in later when the sun was up and placed some toast next to the bed. She sat with Sophie and talked to her about attending a group session that afternoon.

"It might help," she said, "talking to other girls your age who might be going through similar things, who might understand."

The thought of sharing her feelings with others filled Sophie will horror. She picked up the toast but couldn't eat. She curled herself up under the blankets and refused to move. When the doctor came to take her to the meeting, she shouted and spat at him. She tore at her hair and at the bandages on her wrist. She flailed her arms and screamed like a wild animal. She surprised herself. Eventually they sedated her, which was what she had wanted.

The days slid together after that. Light and dark bled into constant twilight. People came and went, the shadow cat came and went. Time and pain and life merged into a comfortable blur. She didn't know how much time passed and she didn't care.

The light hurt her eyes, but she couldn't ignore it. She was awake for the first time in days, maybe weeks. She could see shapes moving in front of her, voices that sometimes seemed close, sometimes far away. She tried to speak but couldn't; tried to move but couldn't. She looked down at her own body. It was covered lightly by a white sheet, but she could see her bones pressing against it. A needle pumped clear liquid into her arm from a machine beside the bed. Slowly the people came into focus. A man in a white coat leaned in towards her, calling her name. Her mother was there, standing too close to the man, peering over his shoulder. Nurse Barton was by the door. Sophie tried to smile at her but the muscles in her face had wasted.

The figures moved away. She heard her mother cry and tried to reassure her, but couldn't get the words out. After they had gone Nurse Barton moved towards the bed. She sat down beside her and stroked her hair.

"Can you hear me, Sophie?"

Sophie nodded and this time she did force something like a smile across her face.

"It's going to be okay, honey. You're going to be okay." Nurse Barton lifted Sophie's arm and pulled back the bandages still firmly attached to her wrist. "These can't heal until you get your strength back."

Suddenly, Sophie wanted to gain her strength; she wanted to be better. She was scared. She had wanted to die before, but now she didn't. Now, for the first time in a long time, the fight for life returned to her. She reached out to Nurse Barton. She knew she had to tell her what had been happening.

"The cat," she whispered.

"The cat? You like cats, don't you?"

Sophie shook her head. "The shadow cat hurts me."

Nurse Barton smiled with pity. "There are no cats here, honey, no animals allowed in the hospital, remember? It must have been a bad dream." She stood to leave but Sophie was desperate to tell her what was happening.

"Cat, cat did this." She held up her arm but Nurse Barton pushed it firmly back down and tucked the sheet over it.

"Shh now, Sophie. Rest now. We'll talk later. I'll come back later."

Sophie closed her eyes. Tears slipped down her cheeks but she was too weak to wipe them away. She had let this happen, made it happen. She knew it was her own fault and now she didn't have the strength to stop it.

The pain woke her. She looked down and the cat crouched beside her; the bandages were pulled down and it lapped and sucked at the open gash. She tried to pull her hand away but the cat hissed at her and bit down harder.

The Grim Keepers

"Leave me alone. Please, leave me alone," she begged.

"Sophie?"

The corridor was as dark as the room but she could make out the figure of Nurse Barton moving towards her from the doorway. She was filled with hope.

"Look," she motioned toward her wrist with her eyes. "The cat, the cat." Nurse Barton closed the door behind her and switched on the lamp by Sophie's bed. The cat stayed where it was, crouched beside her, its claws digging into her arm as its teeth gnawed her flesh.

"There's no cat, honey." Nurse Barton sat beside her, beside the cat, and stroked her hair.

"Can't you see it?"

"There's no cat, Sophie." Nurse Barton stopped stroking Sophie's hair and instead stroked the cat's fur. She kept her eyes on Sophie as she stood up. Her hands closed around the cat's neck and dragged it up so that its feet hung in the air. It didn't struggle.

"There is no cat," Nurse Barton repeated a little louder. "There's only me, Sophie."

Nurse Barton held the cat out in front of her as one hand cradled its body and the other ripped its head off. The cat shuddered as she pulled it apart like an old teddy bear. She held its body up above her and looked at the tattered flesh.

"There, there, little cat," she said as she brought the body towards her and drank from it, its blood dripping down her chin and onto her white uniform. The shadow cat faded in her hands as the blood ran out onto the floor.

Sophie watched frozen with the horror of it, unable to make sense of what was happening. She leaned over the side of the bed, feeling bile burn her throat as she wretched. She turned back to Nurse Barton, and saw that she too had begun to blur and fade into a dark, shifting shape. Sophie dragged herself from the bed, landing heavily on the floor. The shadow swirled and twisted in on itself, collapsing into a smoky pile on the floor beside her—the shadow creature that had once been Nurse Barton seeped past her towards the dark corner and disappeared into the other shadows.

Sophie tried to sit up but her body was weak and broken. She had lost the fight, she knew it now; she was ready to give up. Resting her cheek against the cool floor, she closed her eyes and listened to the deep purr that echoed around her as she slipped away.

The Grim Keepers

About Rachel Fox

Rachel Fox is a Supernatural and Horror writer who lives in London, England. After writing for her own amusement for many years, she started posting her short stories on ABCTales.com, an online community of writers, and to her surprise she found that people liked them.

She recently won the AuthorTrope 'I made the darkness' Halloween writing contest for her short story 'The Exchange', which you can hear brought to life on her website.

Her first novel 'The Herring Hanger' is set for release in December 2015.

Website: www.rachelfox.co.uk
Email: rachelfoxfiction@gmail.com

The Grim Keepers

Darkness Calls
By Charlotte Rose Lange

I slide myself closer to him, abandoning the warm spot I'd created for myself on my half of his bed. He'd been very clear about that. One week into the relationship and we'd already set clear boundaries. Mother would be proud. My nose finds his shoulder, warm and bare. I arch forward until my lips find his neck, then inch upward one kiss at a time until my tongue can reach his endearingly ticklish earlobe.

"Mmph," he says through the dark. "What are you doing?"

I pull away, partially retreating to my no-longer-warm half of his bed.

"Oh, I...thought you'd maybe like to

engage in certain activities."

"It's Tuesday."

"Right." I speed-read through my mental list of the relationship boundaries I'd agreed to. Tuesday was important because...I couldn't remember—probably about how he values his sleep schedule. I sneak my head up to the edge of his pillow. As long as I don't talk I'm not disturbing his sleep, and the sound of his breathing is comforting.

"Ha, don't tell me you're afraid of the dark."

I hesitate to respond. Lies are a surefire way to kill a relationship, but I'm not *afraid*-afraid of the dark. I just don't like it touching me.

I shift my body completely out of his side of the bed, his territory. A hand tunnels under the blankets between us and caresses my own hand. He's not usually so sweet.

"No, of course not," I say. "It's just really dark in here. So dark I can't tell if my eyes are opened or closed. So dark I can feel it closing in. So dark—"

"Save it, Shakespeare. It's after midnight." On our first date I'd been charmed that he called me Shakespeare. I shouldn't have been.

"Oh, okay."

The Grim Keepers

The hand releases mine. I feel the blankets collapse now that the comfy little tunnel connecting him to me has been vacated. From this far away I can't hear his breathing, I can't hear anything. The silence laps at my nerves. Temptation upon temptation urges me to maintain the conversation: a standard "Good night", a corny "See you in the morning", or a pushy "How was your day?"

I hate how big his bed is. I hate how there are no windows and the doorjamb is so tight only a pathetic crumb of light gets through—which is of course smothered with a folded towel. I hate how cold his room is. Everything from the tile to the comforter is ice cold. My one strategy is to move as little as possible to let my own body heat create a warm spot.

I really can't tell if my eyes are open or shut. The all-encompassing black burrows deep into my eye sockets, daring me to hide under the covers, but I'm no longer a child. Cold skitters at my elbows and toes, but I stick to my strategy. Silence murmurs in the corners, pulling at the frayed threads of my imagination.

Anything could be happening inches in front of my face right now I'd have no clue. A tentacle monster gyrating obscenely. A goblin with nails as sharp as needles angling to pop out my eyes, or maybe it'll start with my nails, seeing as it's Tuesday. Evil goo squelching and slurping up the covers, its tiny heart set on sliding across my tongue, down my throat, and into my soul. I bite my lips closed but can't protect my nose.

I sit up suddenly, dispersing my childhood haunts.

"I've got to go to the bathroom. Be right back."

He doesn't answer.

I drag my thighs across the frigid sheets and wince when my feet flop onto the cold, cold tile. Even with my fuzzy socks chills slither up between my toes.

Cold and long, something slips down my left ankle and peels down my sock. Down, down, past my arch, lingering at the ball of my foot, and then off.

I stoop and grasp my bare left foot with both hands. There's no such thing as goblins. My sock must've just snagged on something.

I pat around my foot in a spiral search pattern, all the while screaming 'F-U' to my childish phobia. Nothing is going to latch onto my wrist. I saw this room with the light on earlier. Besides, a tentacle monster, a goblin, and evil goo wouldn't fit under a single bed much less get along. Unless they had reason to.

I curse my imagination and tuck my feet back up on the mattress.

"Do you mind if I turn on the light for a second?"

No answer. Most likely ignoring me instead of sleeping. Even so, I don't want to bug him. I hold my head high, fixate on the mantra, "I am an adult," and march my one-sock feet to where I last saw the door. I miss my mark, but a bit of shuffling around and the clue of the towel guide me to the knob.

I open the door, quick and quiet. I dart out into the blessed low light of the hallway and seal his cursed bedroom behind me.

His house is foreign to me. This is only my second time here and he never advocated exploring. He didn't expressly forbid it either. I grope the wall but the light switch evades me. Maybe there are no light switches in this house, just like there are no rugs. I shuffle forward, comforted by the back and forth sound of my bare foot then my socked foot across tile. I'm tempted to whistle, to fully drive away the silence, but the ridiculous notion that the evil goo hitched a ride on my shoulder makes me hesitate. Better to keep my lips closed. I rationalize my action by thinking there could be a fly or a dangling spider inches from my mouth at this very second.

Pain rips up my calf, originating from my right big toe. I gasp, wide-mouthed, in shock. I clamp my lips shut. Crying out over a little thing like stubbing my toe would not be a good enough reason for waking up the neighborhood, according to him. In brighter news, I've found the steps.

I start with my left, then lift my right. The long and cold nail of Mr. Goblin slides down my ankle, hooking my last sock, tracing my arch, and kissing my throbbing toe. I freeze. I dare not turn and look for the sock. I choose to believe it is at the bottom of the stairs. Fleet steps with high knees carry me to the top of the stairs. On this level the street lights leak in through the blinds, throwing shaking lines of light onto his stacks of medical books. I grab a small throw from the end of the couch and curl up next to the window. Branches and power lines dance a frantic tango in the violent wind.

The storm reminds me of a night over a decade ago. The raging winds took the power out in the whole block. A neighborhood boy two grades above me had crawled through my window, said he knew I'd be scared and too stubborn to tell. He promised to protect me from the dark if I would just hold still.

'What's that tugging at my clothes and tracing up and down?' I'd asked.

'Why, just Mr. Squid,' he'd said. 'Stay quiet.'

'What's that pulling at my hair and pinching here and there?' I'd asked.

'Why, just Mr. Goblin,' he'd said. 'Stay still.'

'What's that oozing about, cold now like evil goo?' I'd asked. He didn't answer. I reached out to him.

He was cold.

'Don't worry,' they said through the dark. 'We've taken care of it. Now off to sleep with you.'

A chill jolts me awake. I pull the throw back onto me and dip back into the memory.

Gramps found him dead in my bed in the morning. Auntie said God struck him down. The police said he got what he deserved and didn't press the issue. No one believed the darkness got him. I'm not a complete fool. A few semesters into college it suddenly dawned on me what Ned would have done had he not died, but no amount of psychotherapy would convince me the dark had nothing to do with his convenient end.

The only school-provided counselor that I didn't think was a complete idiot had told me "the incident" is only as much of an issue as I feel it is. At the time, I wondered if this advice delegitimizes the experiences of those who are more traumatized by such incidents, but for me it clicked. I didn't have to worry that I wasn't reacting to the incident properly and, darkness aside, that was that.

Other counselors insisted my blank dating history is a direct impact of the incident. In part, finally saying yes to a date was a means to prove them wrong—just in part.

Speaking of him, I should get back in bed before I fall asleep here. That would be hard to explain in the morning. With extreme reluctance I poke my bare feet out from the throw and lower them onto the cold, cold—warm and fuzzy? I reach down to the floor and find my socks, fuzzy as always, a bit warm, and ever so slightly damp.

When such things happen—when my keys return themselves to my purse, when the front door locks behind me, when my teacup is fuller than I remember—I find it best not to dwell.

I slip on my socks and shuffle over to the pit of darkness lapping at the top of the stairs. Step

The Grim Keepers

by step, Mr. Goblin and Mr. Squid guide me deeper into the dark, the evil goo watching my back. At the base of the steps, my fingertips trace loops and dips along the smooth wall until the door frame dumps my hand into the open doorway. I shuffle forward, nudging the twisted towel out of the way, expecting to bump into the door any second. My knees hit the edge of his mattress.

I gently reenter my side of his bed and pull up the covers. It's still warm.

A cozy tunnel forms between us. His warmth wraps around my torso and nuzzles the back of my neck.

"Love you," I say, just to say. And in the moment, it may have been true.

The blanket collapses tight against me. Silence blares, coldness grips me, and the immovable dark leans in. I reach out into his territory, my knuckles crack against his cold, still arm. I snuggle in closer, my guilt leaking onto him.

'Why have you done this?' I ask my friends in the dark.

'He would have hurt you in the end. Don't worry. We'll take care of everything.'

I can't see a thing, but I know what they're

doing. Mr. Squid drags the twisted, taut, frayed towel outside and into the trash. Mr. Goblin picks bits of fuzzy sock out of the dead man's mouth. The evil goo slithers up my neck, licks my earlobe, and slides in through my nose—finally snuggling up inside my brain where it was born.

About Charlotte Rose Lange

Charlotte Rose Lange is a freelance editor and writer, who obtained her undergraduate degree in Communications/Social Influence at Edgewood College. She is open to projects in technical writing, specifically board game rulebooks. She is currently working on her young adult novel 'Ascendant': When a young witch harbors a newly ascended being who broke the rules, she's thrust into a world of high magics and higher consequences.

Linkedin:
https://www.linkedin.com/pub/charlotte-rose-lange/78/b19/511

Evil Eye
By AJ Millen

Georgia breathed a sigh of exhausted relief as she laid her beautiful baby girl gently in the cot. Big blue eyes blinked sleepily up at her then closed as the child finally settled into the deep rhythms of sleep. Georgia fingered the gaudy stone at her throat and said a prayer to the god she didn't believe in that her daughter would never know humiliation like she had when growing up.

The necklace had been placed around her neck by her superstitious Greek grandmother, Yiayia Gogo, on her twelfth birthday. It was, she had said, to protect her from the Evil Eye—the *mati*—but also carried a special charm that would protect others, too.

The Grim Keepers

"I know you think this is all Greek stupidity, my darling," she had said. *"But I know. You have your Aunt Voula's eyes, powerful eyes, and there lies the danger."*

Georgia had laughed as she thought of her sweet great-aunt in the village of Gogo's island home. Her tired, benevolent gaze through rheumy blue eyes seemed anything but powerful or dangerous to her.

"Go on, you laugh," her grandmother had said. *"But even if you don't believe, wear it always. Please, as a favor to your granny."*

Years of living abroad since coming to England as a young bride in the 1960s had done nothing to erase Gogo's stubborn village upbringing. Her belief in the Evil Eye—a curse thought to be cast by those with blue eyes, intentionally or innocently—was unshakable. So, too, was her conviction that the gaudy talisman would neutralize the evil as long as the sender or receiver of the *mati* kept it close to their heart.

In spite of her Mediterranean genes, Georgia was born and bred in suburban Britain and not given to such superstition. But she loved her eccentric Greek grandmother and hated to see disappointment in her eyes.

So she had promised.

The Grim Keepers

Every day, she wore the pea-sized stone, the color of a blue Lego brick with a creepy-looking eyeball crudely painted on it. Even when the mean girls at school, who never missed the chance to mock her for her weight, her lack of grace, her love of books, and lack of boyfriends spotted the bauble hidden beneath her shirt as they changed for gym. Mercilessly, they had honed in on something new, something different, something distinctly odd that could be used to torment their victim. Then one day, in a hissy fit of teenage rebellion, Georgia slipped it off and hid it with the broken nibs and old shavings at the bottom of her pencil case.

Lucy and the other girls had waited for her at the school gates that afternoon. Faster and stronger than her, it was nothing for them to take her bag and empty the contents onto the muddy verge in a fit of cackling glee, trampling Georgia's drawings underfoot. They found her necklace, drawing it out of the pencil case like it was a piece of snot on a string and screeching with laughter at its primitive gaze. Hot shame and anger flushed Georgia's cheeks, and she felt a shock, like a bolt of unseen lightning, as she glared at Lucy strutting along the side of the road and pretending to model the eye pendant like it was the crown jewels.

The Grim Keepers

Something shifted inside Georgia's mind. A faint smell of singed hair stained the air. Her eyes burned with frustration and hatred as she glared at her tormentors.

Lucy tripped and fell back into the path of a speeding lorry. A scream, the screech of brakes, a sickening thud, and a tinkle on the pavement resounded as Georgia's necklace landed on the cement next to her. A slick stream of red trickled into the gutter.

It had been the last time Georgia ever took her necklace off.

She shook herself away from her childhood memory, again burying the horror of what she knew she had done, although everyone insisted it was just an awful freak accident. It had been years since she allowed herself to think of that day. The tiredness that came with being a new mother must have let her defenses down.

Tonight had been particularly tough. Sam was working a double shift, and Georgia's mum had refused to come anywhere near the baby until she had shaken her latest bout of flu. So, of course, the baby had screamed the house down for five solid hours. Nothing Georgia did calmed her. Not hugs, not milk, not bouncing up and down or singing every lullaby in the bilingual book. She

The Grim Keepers

felt like an utter failure as a mother until suddenly, without warning, the scarlet-faced infant stopped her bawling and surrendered abruptly to an exhausted sleep, deep, regular breathing interrupted only by the occasional shudder of leftover sobs.

Finally, a chance to breathe and to wipe the baby sick off her blouse.

She stripped to her bra in the bathroom and wet a flannel to wipe her chest clean. There was semi-digested milk caught on her pendant, clogging up the link connecting the stone to the chain. Carefully, she pulled it over her matted hair. Just as she was about to run it under the tap, a piercing squeal rang out from the baby's room.

Georgia dropped everything, curling into a ball and banging her head repeatedly against the wall behind her as she slapping her hands over her ears. The screaming continued.

"What? What now?" she screamed. "What the hell is wrong now? Can't you please—for the love of God—please, just stop?"

With a shock of electricity, she spied the blue bead blurred through her desperate tears, dangling over the edge of the sink. She scrambled to her feet, reaching for the talisman like a drowning woman clutching at a buoyancy aid. But too late.

Horror ran through her veins like ice as the baby's crying suddenly stopped.

She knew, with absolute certainty, that her prayer had been answered. Her daughter never would suffer the humiliation she had known as a teenager.

She would never do anything at all.

About AJ Millen

Words have been AJ Millen's friends since she was a child growing up in England. She started telling her own stories young, and she's still at it. After school, she became a news reporter and later went into press and public relations. Everything changed in 1989 when she took a six-month working holiday in Greece. That was the plan—until a brown-eyed boy in Samos persuaded her to stay. Today, he is her husband and father to their 18-year-old son.

AJ Millen lives in Athens, works in Corporate Communications, and writes short stories and general burblings for her blog:

http://shemeanswellbut.blogspot.com

Lethal
By Jason Pere

"Just one more," Steven said as he shut the door to his locker and slipped the combination lock back into place. His working day was done and it was time for him to go home. He lingered there for a considerable length of time, unable to move. Steven tried to keep from shaking. He was jittery. He had killed a man today. Steven had killed many men. It was part of his job as a correctional officer for the great state of Texas to kill men who had been sentenced to die.

At first it didn't bother him. There was even a certain mystique about being on the Death Team. There were a few sick cases that put in for the job because they wanted to get away with ending the life of another human being. Steven was not one of those; he was just looking for the pay grade bump for a C.O Class Three to a C.O Class Four. Getting Death Team certified was the fastest way he'd been able to achieve that next step in his career. He could stomach the duty and carry the weight of it for years, seemingly unburdened. He practiced a sort of ignorance when he was called to end the life of an inmate. Steven's body was present in the Death Room and his hands did their assigned task each time, but his mind was always miles away. This was how he lived with what he had to do. He just kept the reality of his actions from conscious thought. It was how he had made it nineteen years as a Correctional Officer and it was how he planned to make it to his twentieth year and then finally retire.

Steven may have been able to keep what he did locked away during the daylight hours, but when he slept, his dreams would not spare him. They forced him to remember the images he suppressed and to recall the torment that took place in the Death Room. The weight weighing Steven down had begun to take its toll, whether the man would acknowledge it or not. For months now he had fought the shaking in his body that gripped him each time an inmate was sent up the row. He told himself, "Just one more. Just one more," under his breath. It was the mantra he had begun to recite after flipping the switches on the machines today. He was only scheduled for one more execution before retirement. Steven clung to that fact as a light at the end of the tunnel.

The dreams were beginning to feel so genuine. Steven was not sure how much more he could take. He had tried everything to help get a restful night's sleep—alcohol to black him out, caffeine to keep him awake, even pills from the doctor, but nothing worked. His last hope was that leaving this place behind him for good would be enough to make the dreams stop once and for all. Steven couldn't spend the rest of his days seeing the faces of the men he had killed every time he closed his eyes.

He zipped up his jacket and grabbed his duffel bag as he left the locker room behind. Steven quickly walked through the corridors of the prison and avoided any interaction with the other guards there. He just wanted to get home and be done with the day. He was able to quickly check out through each of the security stations and get to his jeep. Once inside his vehicle, the familiar smell of the pine air freshener and feel of the seat helped to calm him. The greatest comfort to the man was the promise of home and a proper meal before bed. "Just one more," Steven said as he turned the key in the ignition.

He was grateful for the lack of traffic on the way home. There hardly seemed to be any other cars on the road at all, and he made every green light on the way, to boot. He started to feel pretty good about his chances at a nice, relaxing evening when he remembered his refrigerator and pantry were absolutely bare. This upset him, because the knowledge that he had no worthwhile sustenance at home only served to remind him just how hungry he really was. Steven could hear his belly rumbling with its demand for food. He thought for a moment to pull off at the supermarket and grab something out of the freezer section like he normally would in this situation, but today had been a hard day and he needed something more than a spartanly topped pizza.

Steven counted his blessings that his belly had made its desires known before he got too much further down the road. He could still make a small detour and stop in at his favorite bar and grill, Jack's Lone Star. The beer there was cold and always had a nice head on it, and the kitchen fare was surprisingly tasty for a place that looked like a dive bar on the outside. Steven about kicked himself for not thinking to stop at Jack's from the start. He knew he would be able to get the kind of meal he needed to put the day behind him. It would be worth the extra twenty minutes out of the way.

The jeep pulled up into a premium parking space right next to the Lone Star's front door. Steven stepped out of his ride and took a moment to feel the cool breeze blowing in off of the range. He regarded the overly tacky neon sign and its humongous blinking yellow star. It was so tasteless it was wonderful. Steven made his way inside the bar. Jack's was fairly calm for a Friday night. It looked like they were doing good business but the ambiance was not nearly the blaring country jukebox, mechanical bull flinging frat boys left and right, off-key karaoke, and drunken foolery Steven had anticipated.

He honed in on a desirable seat at the corner of the bar furthest from the restrooms and proceeded to stake his claim. He sat and all his aches and pains of the day seemed to fade away into the bar stool beneath him. He had not felt this good in a long time. Clearly, coming to Jack's had been the right call. Steven allowed himself a mental pat on the back for his wisdom.

Not more than a minute after sitting down

the bartender came to serve him. The Corrections Officer marveled at how fast the service was tonight. He could not ever recall being taken care of so quickly in twenty years of frequenting Jack's Lone Star. It looked to be more and more his night every second. *Perhaps I'll get a good night's sleep after all,* Steven thought.

"What can I get you, buddy?" asked the bartender. Steven was surprised. He hadn't noticed it at first, but the man behind the bar was not Jack. Jack always worked on a Friday.

"Just give me the biggest glass of the coldest thing you got on tap," Steven said. "Jack on vacation or something?" he pried.

"Oh, no, he just needed me to come in tonight is all. You need him for something?" said the bartender as he placed a frosty glass of beer in front of Steven. There was something familiar about this man, but he couldn't put a finger on it.

"No, just figured he would be in on a Friday. He always is. Can I see the after-hours menu, please?"

"Do you want the regular menu? We still have a full kitchen. Anything you want."

"What? When did that happen? Is something special going on tonight?"

"New cook and new menu. He's real good

on that grill back there. He can whip up damn near anything."

Steven thought hard for a moment. It seemed like something had smiled on him, and his night was rapidly becoming a memorable occasion. He took a long sip of the glass in front of him and then had to take another sip immediately. It was some of the best-tasting beer he had had in a long time. "Anything you say. Well, you know, I have a hankering for a cheesesteak sandwich and some steak fries. All-time favorite meal, right there. Can your boy do that?" Steven asked.

"Cheesesteak and fries, no problem. Out in the quick for you, sir."

Steven was sure he knew the bartender from somewhere. He knew it was bad form, but his curiosity could not wait any longer. "Sorry there, but I have to ask, have we met before?" he blurted out as the bartender turned to leave.

"No need to be sorry, buddy. I'd tell you if we had met before. I'm sure you would remember me. I'm just that kind of person," he said with an enormous smile. He turned and went to put in Steven's order with the kitchen.

Steven sat sipping the earth-shatteringly good beverage in his hand and searched his memory. *He must just have one of those faces, I suppose,* he thought to himself.

"Is there anything you would like to say to me, son?" came a voice from over Steven's shoulder. He turned to look at the speaker and was dumbfounded to see a priest standing behind him.

"Excuse me, sir. Not to be rude, but I think you might be in the wrong place," Steven said after the initial shock wore off.

"Not to be rude, either, but I think I'm right where God needs me to be. Now, was there anything you wanted to say to me?"

"What makes you think I have anything to say to you?"

"You just look like you have a lot on your mind."

"I think I'll be fine on my own."

"You sure about that, son?"

"Yes, I'm sure about that."

"Order's up. Here's your food, buddy," came the voice of the bartender. Steven turned to look as the man put down a savory, creamy, steaming-hot cheesesteak sandwich, a side of perfectly golden steak fries, and a fresh glass of whatever that amazing brew was.

"Thank you," Steven said. He was about to dig into his food when he got the sense that he knew the priest from somewhere as well. He looked back at where the other man had been standing, but he was no longer there. Steven returned his attention to his meal and ate. It was amazing; the food tasted not of this earth. Steven took his time and relished each bite down to the very last crumb. He swore it was not possible for food to taste this good. He had to stop himself from nearly licking the plate.

After he was done he sat and reveled in the pleasure of a full belly. He was interrupted when the bartender placed yet another towering glass of that divine drink in front of him. "Oh, I think I'm at my limit here. I already had two tall ones," Steven said.

"Oh, I thought I heard you say just one more. I must have misunderstood," said the bartender with an apologetic look in his eyes.

Steven had not realized he'd been speaking. *Have I been saying that the whole time?* he thought, feeling a little surge of panic creep into his mind. He looked at the glass and craved to drink it down. He had driven farther and in worse shape before. Steven knew that a third drink might put him over the legal limit but it would not put him over his tolerance. "What the hell. I won't tell if you don't," he said with a devilish grin.

The Grim Keepers

"Lips are sealed, buddy."

Steven enjoyed nursing his drink along. About halfway down he waved the bartender back over. "I'd like to settle up, now."

The bartender looked Steven up and down before he spoke. "Jack said you would be in tonight and that your tab would be on the house."

Steven was taken aback. He knew Jack had always taken care of his regulars but this was never something he would have expected. Before Steven could say anything else, the bartender spoke again.

"He also said strawberry shortcake was your favorite and that you could use a piece." He quickly produced a plate from behind the bar with a picture-perfect piece of strawberry shortcake on it.

"Thank you. And tell Jack thank you," was all Steven could say.

"You can thank ol' Jack yourself when you see him next." The bartender nodded and left.

Steven finished his drink and the scrumptious dessert in front of him and then made his way to his jeep. The ride home from the Lone Star was quick. Steven could feel his eyes growing heavy and his body beginning to shut down for the night. If ever there was a chance for a peaceful sleep it would be tonight. "Just one more," Steven said as he slipped the key into the lock of his front door. He moved through his darkened house up to his bedroom as fast as his weary feet would carry him. He opened the door and walked inside.

A blast of light hit him as he entered his bedroom. After his eyes adjusted to the brightness, he struggled to reconcile with what he saw before him. He did not stand in his bedroom. He was in the prison—the Death Room, but it was much bigger than he remembered. It had to be, because it was filled with every inmate he had ever executed. They all looked at him, their skin cold and grey, but their eyes burned with hatred and anger. In the middle of the room where the execution table was supposed to be, Steven saw his bed.

He wanted to scream. This was impossible. This could not be real. It had to be a bad dream— it had to be. He looked at the dead men assembled in the room and felt like his mind had come unraveled. To Steven's right was the bartender. His name was George Tubal. Steven had put a needle in his arm six years ago for eight counts of first degree murder. On his left was the priest. His name was Father Patrick Murdock. He was one of the last inmates sentenced to the electric chair at the prison before it was decommissioned. He had been found guilty of abusing and molesting more than a dozen children. Right in front of Steven was Jack. He had been the first man Steven had ever killed. Jack had set his wife on fire as well as the man with whom she'd had an affair.

In perfect unison, every one of the dead men in the room spoke. "Just one more." They chanted it over and over again. Steven shook with fright. He felt a hand touch him on the shoulder. He turned and what he saw nearly made him catatonic. The man who had placed a hand on his shoulder was himself, dressed in a perfectly pressed and cleaned uniform. Steven looked into his own eyes. The version of him that had just appeared in the room brought his face within mere inches of his terrified doppelganger and spoke. "Just one more." The Steven dressed in uniform forced the cowering man onto the bed in the middle of the room. When the horrified Steven finally lay flat, he looked to see that he did not lay on his bed but on the execution table. He felt the hands of many long-dead men strap him down and the needle pierce the skin of his arm. Steven screamed until his eyes finally closed. He never had bad dreams again.

About Jason Pere

Jason self-published his first novel 'Modern Knighthood: Diary of a Warrior Poet' in 2012, and has continued to pursue self-publishing with his sophomore novel 'Calling the Reaper: First Book of Purgatory'. Jason discovered CWC early on in 2015 and has been a passionate member since, diving into multiple collaborative fiction projects with other CWC authors. When not writing or enduring his "Real World Job" Jason enjoys Netflix time with his family, breaking out obscure board games and dorking out with friends, firing up the his game console and surviving a Zombie Apocalypse, or indulging in baked goods and sleep.

The Grim Keepers

Remus
By Tony Stark

It was always two days before the first frost of the season that I arose.

When the sun was high and children played on the beaches near Blackpool, I hid away in my lassitude, buried deep under the old, brick storm drains of the ancient city. I had lived in Lancashire for nearly six-hundred years, lingering in many of the abandoned mines or the deepest, wildest forests while the summer of the year raged above me. Once the days finally began to wane and the nights grew chill and cold, I could finally bear to leave the shelter of the cold earth and its gnarled trees and walk by night amongst the meadows.

The Grim Keepers

It had been so very long since I had seen the trees, green and fresh with leaf and life. I could not bear to even look outside when the summer raged, so fierce and impressive. To me, ever since the Incident, trees had been robed in gold and scarlet, brown and beige, wearing their fading green leaves as ornaments of the yang time of year fading away. The frosts came, and I would emerge in time to see the flats and shops adorned with decorations for All Hallow's Eve and Guy Fawkes Day. This was my morning, these spooky days of mystery. This was my first real glimpse of the year, the time of revels, bonfires, and celebration of the death of a traitor. It was fitting.

I settled in the Angel Isle, as it was called back then, in the time of the first Roman settlement of London. I had lived a wretched existence, hiding in the catacombs under the city which bore my brother's name, lurking for all but the very heel of the year in darkness. When the Christians came and supplanted the older worshippers whose caves I shared, they welcomed me as yet another of their shabby, destitute poor— another friend of their crucified Lord, Jeshua. Needing as little sustenance as I did after the Incident, their shared meals of bread, fish, and wine were more than I had eaten since the time I once laughed too often, too merrily, at my brother's lazy ways. When the Romans, with their massive roads and intensive control, took the wildlands of the Island of England, they brought back fine, warm wool and tales of a hyperborean world so far to the north that the summer days stretched wildly long. The winter days squished so thin and pale, the sun barely penetrated through the mists and fogs and snows.

It sounded like absolute heaven to me. I implored my Christian colleagues to assist me in my journey, and they readily did, so eager were they to bring the message of their resurrected Lord to the isle. I hid under blankets and skins and travelled in the heel of the year, just as the festival of Saturnalia was beginning in the streets my brother had laid out so many ages ago. It was a long journey and a dangerous one. But the Alps in the north of Italia masked the sun into blissfully short days and long, shadowed twilights—the first relief I had felt from the wild dance of the sun since my killer had murdered me on the hills of Rome. Beyond the line of the mountains, as the rumor had said, the sun grew fainter and weaker. The snows—the glorious, cold, stately snows—grew deeper, and for the first time since I had been murdered I actually felt *strong*.

161

The Grim Keepers

When my feet first touched the jagged, limestone rocks along the shore of England, I felt a strong, magical presence comfort my wasted bones and flesh. I took in a breath of air—chill and cold, damp and filled with the eternal, quiet strength of yin. My companion, a preacher from the people of the Fish, turned and looked at me with wonder.

"Why, Remus," he had said, "your cheeks bear the bloom of life in them!"

At first, I was grateful to be farther north than I had ever been, far away from the constant tumult of the city my brother Romulus had founded with his aggressive, implacably hungry energy. But as the years wound on, I noticed that the suns of summer would burn and drive me deep into the limestone caverns cut out by the sea of the coast. I moved ever northward, first through the deep forests of the Danelaw in East Anglia and then, finally, to the coalfields of Lancashire, which even then were being worked for their black ores. There I found equilibrium, a bearable state of hiding from the height of summer without being wasted by it and *living* amongst my fellow man without being exhausted by it. Perhaps it was the vast fields of coal, so cold and still and yin like me, with a great potential lying dormant through death. Or perhaps I just found the right latitude at last. But the rolling hills and rivers of Lancashire became my home. I came to know every cave, every deep wood, every dark place in the countryside.

During the dark half of the year, I grew to know the people of the country as well. I walked amongst them and took odd jobs as a teacher and a tutor. I passed from generation to generation amongst them, coming to know their ways and their customs. A great fondness for these plain-spoken, hard-working folk grew in me. In their toils in the coalmines and the fields, I saw a certain similarity to my own harsh, bitter, and lonely existence. Perhaps it was because this happened at my first real emergence for the year, but the joyful cries and petitioning for gifts at All Hallows' Eve seemed to me the best time of all for these simple people. Their house-to-house begging for victuals, clad in strange and disguising garb, was again so similar to my own story.

I had come to call this place my home, wandering the streets in the excitement-filled days before the end of October, watching the families I had observed for centuries preparing for autumn with faces and hands so similar to those of their forebears. I had found peace here, albeit an outsider's peace.

I was excited to find, that year, that the turning of the leaves came earlier, the frosts sooner and harsher, than in many a year. I could enter the world of men before October even came, so I could visit with my friends who had grown another year older and more tired but were still joyous and happy people in spite of it. I was grateful for the auspicious early yin; the summer had been late in coming as well and I faced an ability to spend more days in the world than I had in centuries.

I had forgotten completely about my brother, the manic despot who had founded the martial city of Rome.

It therefore came as some surprise when, one night not long before Hallows' Eve, I saw my brother on the television. I sat in a pub with some coalminers when the evening news announced several ancient, closed coal seams had been purchased by an American Tycoon. I didn't pay the story much heed—those matters were not for the likes of the dead—but one of my friends pointed at the map of Lancashire on the screen, exposing the dangers of the sale.

"Those seams were closed for a reason!"

he called out to the pub at large, met by a chorus of agreement. "They run too deep. They cut too far into England. No matter what 'new-fangled technology' that rich bastard Flush might be bringing, if they cut any more coal out of those seams, it'll spell subduction and collapse for most of Lancashire!"

"Oh, aye," came the general reply.

"My great-grandfather worked those seams," another man said. "He told me the same thing. They went too deep as it was. That's why no one can make new construction in the northern end of town."

"There's the smug bastard now!" Another pointed at the television as a chorus of boos and a few wadded-up napkins launched toward the screen.

I looked up and beheld my brother's face. I had not considered the possibility Romulus was still alive. Having had such a violent life that he stole my own to add to his bursting coffer, I realized I had come to think that at some point it must have run out. I thought he must have died at some point and passed out of the world. Yet here he was, his effulgently solid bulk crammed into a very expensive businessman's suit, his corpulent neck spilling over his white collar. His eyes were black as they always had been, but had shrunk and lay sunken now against a mass of flesh, blotchy and livid with the stains of too much life crammed into a single vessel. He spoke and it was English, but his voice still had the same arrogant, harsh grating it had had as he laughed over my corpse that day so long ago. His words puffed out of him, steaming on the screen, while he wrapped his immense woolen coat closer around him to keep away the slender fingers of chill.

I watched the broadcast, shivering in my bereft body, seized by waves of deathly yin energy striving imperceptibly against my brother, my killer. I looked around at the faces of my friends, the great-great-great-grandchildren of the friends I had had long before. I thought about the heedless way Romulus had always conducted his affairs, wanting what he wanted no matter the cost to others—or to nature. He must have heard about the probable result of resuming this coalmining, and continued regardless. After all this time, he still thought he was immune.

Perhaps he was not immune any longer. I wondered, as I watched my long-estranged brother shivering with the damp drizzle that fell on the screen, if the past year with its weak summer had weakened him. I wondered, as I looked at his blotchy and crapulent face, if the long years of excess living had weakened him further, making him susceptible to the creeping hand of cold, wintry death. I watched him turn on his heel as a reporter quizzed him about the dangers of the mining scheme. He walked into the Savoy Hotel, a Lancashire landmark. I knew he would be lurking in the penthouse suite; he always liked to be the highest, so long as he didn't have to work for it personally.

"How long is Mr. Flush supposed to be in town?" I asked the room in general.

"I hear he's here until Christmas, at least," one of the men said. Another agreed, citing gossip his sister-in-law had revealed from her work at the Savoy.

I nodded, smiled at another friend who proffered me a packet of American Halloween candy. I turned the wrapper over and over in my long, thin, cold fingers, thinking about America, the place that had, until lately, been my brother's home. Thinking about the way he shivered as he proclaimed his intention of laying waste to my home and to the lives of my friends. Thinking about how there were large access tunnels that opened into the basement of the Savoy, ones I had used in the bright time of the year to raid their

The Grim Keepers

kitchens and dustbins for the scraps of food I needed to live.

I thought about all this, about how there would be jovial chaos on the streets next week with a large and raucous party outside the Savoy. I thought about how staffs were thin on All Hallows' Eve, and security was distracted by the bands of children who came 'round to all the downtown shops and hotels. I thought about how, at this most festive time of year, it was about time I paid my poor, shivering, enterprising brother his final visit.

All Hallows' Eve dawned paler and drearier than it had in many turns of the year. I awoke in the storm drains beneath the Savoy Hotel, where I had been sleeping every day since my resolution had formed itself. I stopped in at the pub every night to catch the evening news and noted that, as each day went by with me sleeping beneath him, my brother grew more fraught and exhausted. Perhaps it was from the constant haranguing of the determined locals, loath to let this foreign billionaire come in and ruin their homes. Perhaps it was from the weather, so chill and dreary—quintessential English weather that seemed to dampen and ebb the endless fires in my brother's belly. Perhaps, I thought as I smiled

The Grim Keepers

quietly to myself, it was because the yin which Romulus had thrust upon me now lay closer to him than it had been in millennia.

I made, therefore, a point of spending most evenings and mornings under the Savoy. I would have ventured up into its floors of finery had I not wanted to spoil my opportunity to pass unnoticed on All Hallows' Eve. I returned to the pub every night and watched the blotchiness turn to pallor, watched those black, thankless eyes grow more fretful and anxious with every new interview.

I wondered if he thought of me. I wondered if my brother had some inkling that the sibling he had killed on the hill so long ago was in some way responsible for this sudden illness in him. So long ago had it been, his crime so sudden and thoughtless, I wondered if he thought about me at all. We had each undertaken to build our keeps, from which we would inspire the hearts of men to greatness, each in our own way on those hills of Italy. Romulus had boasted and crowed for months about the formidable castle wall he was to build first around his demesne; he had always been preoccupied with war, invasion, and conquest. I laughed at him about his preoccupations; I didn't take his piratical ways seriously then, back when I was alive. I suppose it was that lack of gravity in the face of Romulus and his rapacious appetites that led to my own demise. More importantly, however, it was because Romulus could never stand to be the butt of a joke.

Not even one of his own making. I had reluctantly decided to build a wall around my kingdom, mostly to keep Romulus from mocking it mercilessly and decrying my realm by doomsaying its swift and complete conquest without any noticeable defenses. I had carried stones from the Tiber up the hill with my long legs and placed them with my wiry arms, one upon the other, until at last the wall I had built was as tall as my arms could reach, which was quite tall—I had always been the thinner and more skyward of the pair of us.

On the appointed day, we met at my hill to examine our work thus far. I was eager to show my brother who, for all his stormy and tempestuous tempers, was still my best friend, the work I had completed. I was proudest of the layout of the city, with its large communal area where my people could gather and celebrate life together. We didn't get past the outer wall.

I could tell this structure, stretching two or three feet over his head, had displeased my brother. His ruddy, doughy face grew more russet as he looked up at the stones that had been so easy for me to place. He strode up and down its perimeter, testing vaguely for weakness. His mood darkened when he found none. I grew concerned as I watched him; I knew I had angered him in some way but at the time, naïve as I was, I did not know how.

He refused to enter the wall to look at what I thought was the true accomplishment of the city. He reluctantly followed me back to his building site, trailing behind me as my long legs easily closed the distance to his city.

Romulus was still coming up the rise behind me as I beheld his construction. He had done very little to manifest his building plan; the innate lassitude of his character had beaten out the megalomaniacal desire. Before me was a half-finished wall that only came up to my admittedly tall bellybutton. The stones of the ramshackle wall had been placed lazily without regard for structural integrity.

I stared down at it. So, this was Rome, the great fortress. This was the wall about which I had been hearing so very much.

Then I made my fatal mistake. I laughed.

To me, it was a light-hearted, surprised

exclamation. I certainly meant no harm. I opened my mouth to ask my brother if he wanted my help to finish his wall when I felt the knife in my back. Romulus had crested the hill in time to hear my laughter and after the shame of his accomplishment and the shock of my own, it had been the final straw.

He stabbed me and stabbed me and finally, as I lay bleeding the last life I ever had onto his soil, he choked the rest of it out of me. His black eyes glowed with hatred, his thick hands strong and relentless.

Needless to say, I hadn't seen him since. He had left me there to wash his hands in the river. As the sun set, the spirits of the dead had come and taken me away, a merciful act of pity so Romulus could not defile me further when he returned. I wondered if he had thought anything about how his brother had disappeared, if he ever imagined I had lingered on as a ghost or a spirit, let alone in this deathly corporeal form. I liked to think that maybe he did, now that the cold and miserable yin year chilled him even in his luxurious penthouse.

I waited underneath him, a spirit of the cold earth, sapping his lusty strength until All Hallows' was finally upon us.

The Grim Keepers

It was, of course, the day when the spirits of the dead could return and visit the living. Surely Romulus was aware he should be expecting company as the night drew its inky cloak around the towering hotel.

I had even less problem than I thought making my way to the penthouse. The employees were preoccupied, as predicted, by the festivities and I had become a familiar and harmless face about the place. No one noticed as my thin hand took a keycard off the front desk; no one cared when I slipped into the secured elevator to the penthouse.

I had planned my ingress well. As the elevator climbed, I set the manual stop for a moment. I removed the light bulbs in the ceiling fixture, leaving the cube in complete darkness. I had a way of melting into darkness, travelling into shadows cast about rooms. It would give me a chance to enter unnoticed, if not unexpected.

I knew I would have very little time. I had to erode the light and the yang in the room if I was to get a proper chance at him. The elevator was a start.

Setting the elevator in motion again, I half closed my eyes and let the yin-ness of the dark bleed into me.

The Grim Keepers

The doors opened and light streamed into the elevator. I saw my brother for the first time since my own murder.

He looked up and his eyes grew wide, even in his bloated face, with terror. The sight of an unwarranted elevator opening on Hallows' Eve, black and abandoned, would alarm anyone. I could tell by the quiver in his cruelly over-sensuous lip that he worried the elevator was not abandoned at all, and that its occupant was his long-deceased brother.

I smiled and closed my eyes. Two of the lights in the room, ones closest to me, popped and went out. Sudden shadows cast into the penthouse, and into those I crept, silent, unnoticed save for the cold breath of air moving with me.

Romulus called out in his harsh voice. "Who's there? Who's in the elevator?" As he did so, he crept toward the gaping elevator, instinctively keeping to the illuminated parts of the room.

His preoccupation with the open door made it easy for me to sneak around to the patio. I wanted as much of the cold Hallows' Eve air as possible inside this absurdly opulent penthouse. I flung the French doors wide open and an obligingly damp, ominous fog blew into the room,

174

puffing out the curtains to perfect effect.

Romulus turned and stared at the patio behind him. Immediately, his teeth chattered. His black eyes suddenly became ringed in white. His hands shook. With no small effort, he managed to press the elevator button hard enough to make the doors close. His focus distracted, I moved in behind him, my soundless, dead feet lithe on the thick carpet.

He watched as the doors shut, locking him into his ornate lodgings. "I know it's you," he whispered to the marble-lined doors. "You can't scare me."

Another, more-living man might have quipped a quip at that point, something along the lines of, "I'm not trying to scare you. I'm trying to kill you." A more powerful and actually evil dead spirit might have done something impressive and visceral at that point to pique his victim's fear.

As for me, being so close to my brother, my killer, after all this time, made me decide something in my heart. He was huge, bloated with his own ego two times the life energy he should have had. He was old; he failed in his resolve and had certainly been guilty of mind. He was, for his gabardine suits and his high-handed tactics, a wretched thing after all—more wretched, in fact, than I. I had my friends, hard-working people. I had the night. I had the moon and the stars. He had only this incredibly expensive bastion from which he could hide from the many, many multitudes who hated and resented him.

Another, more compassionate man might have taken his brother by the hand and led him to the sofa for a long overdue heart-to-heart.

I merely fastened my long fingers tight around my brother's neck and jaw, twisting round and up with all my cold, dead might. I felt the bones in his neck give way and let the immense weight fall from my grip—finally. I had neither desire nor need to announce my presence or my intent. I would leave the proclamations for the living—tonight was the night for the dead to settle accounts.

About Anthony Stark

Anthony Stark is a writer and publisher. He is a paramedic and has a background in engineering and the sciences. His latest novel is 'An Incident in El Noor'. He has also been published in *Tales From Space*, *Sleuth Magazine,* and *Starklight Anthologies*. You can find him at: www.starklightpress.com

The Grim Keepers

Resident 7K
By Rachael Steele

Meaghan's new home was on the sixth floor of a
brick 1939 building. By how slowly the elevator
moved one could be mistaken in thinking it was a
lot higher. Every time the doors opened to her
floor, she noticed the hallway always seemed so
eerily quiet. Having lived here for two months,
Meaghan had yet to see a neighbor. Pushing open
the heavy brown door, she threw her keys down
onto the breakfast nook and kicked off her heels.
She liked this new apartment and hoped she'd stay
here a bit longer than the last place.

Pulling down the wall bed, she could hear
the wind rattling the windows panes. A bolt of
lightning jolted across the sky, knocking her

The Grim Keepers

backwards into the armchair with fright.

"What's going on with me? She murmured. "Why am I so jumpy?"

Reaching for the window ledge, Meaghan pulled herself out of the chair, her eyes peering just over the high sill. Through the blackness she could see the apartment building beside hers; only a few windows were lit. A second bolt of lightning slit the sky, followed by growls of thunder and raining suddenly spitting at the window with a vengeance.

Pulling the curtains closed she went to the bathroom and brushed her teeth. *Hopefully this will pass over before my Halloween party on Saturday. Nobody likes wet candy.* She smirked at her reflection in the mirror.

Rolling over to look at the time, 3am blared out from the alarm clock. Meaghan thought the thunder had woken her until she realized it was the upstairs neighbor and his heavy boots. Ever since she had moved in, all she ever heard from above were heavy boots and slamming doors plus the creaking of the bed springs. The ritual repeated most nights. Tonight, the boots seemed to be shuffling, going backwards and forwards across the maple oak floors above. He groaned in

180

time with the scraping of whatever he moved.

Something heavy hit the floor. Sitting bolt upright, a shudder went down Meaghan's spine. A creaking door, more shuffling, more groaning. Then the door slammed shut. The footsteps shuffled back towards his front door, still dragging something.

Not realizing she had been holding her breath, Meaghan fell back onto the bed, gasping for air. She forced herself to calm down before the irritation got to her, but she jumped out of bed and grabbed her robe. *Surely, he's just moving furniture*, she thought. Opening the front door just enough to get a clear view of the elevator, she waited for it to descend. She could hear the doors shudder open and the sound of the man's boots stepping inside the elevator with the dragging noise behind him. Another crack of lighting snapped through the sky, causing her to jump back against the cold brick wall. The elevator doors clanged shut, and she stood there waiting for it to slowly descend past her floor.

Wrapping her arms tightly around her stomach, she felt herself getting nauseous. The small circular window in the elevator would only align with its counterpart on her floor for a few seconds. She knew there wouldn't be much to see, but felt compelled to look. As the light came down, all she saw was a man wearing a blue hat, his eyes hidden by the brim. She quickly retreated into her apartment, slamming the door behind her.

At least I can have some peace and quiet now he's gone out, she thought. Pulling the duvet up to her ears, she listened to the wind as it whipped the leaves off the trees and left behind the dry, cracked branches that now creaked outside her bedroom window.

The next morning, Meaghan felt so tired. She reluctantly got ready for work and made the extra effort to stop by the trash room to drop off her recycling. Absently sorting plastic from cardboard, she stopped abruptly as something caught her eye. An object jutted out from under the large cardboard boxes, and she turned slowly to try to make it out. Dropping the recycling bag, she crept towards it, her heart pounding in her ears.

"This is crazy. What the hell am I doing looking at other people's trash?" she whispered.

She couldn't help herself; she tugged on the object crudely wrapped in black plastic. It was haphazardly held together by a thin, dirty yellow rope. Removing a steel nail file from her bag, she punctured one of the corners, peeling it slowly back to reveal a faded blue rug beneath. Hearing footsteps stop on the concrete outside, she looked over her shoulder at the door, praying silently for whoever it was to walk past. The shadow of feet was just visible from where she squatted. The person standing outside the door rummaged around in their bag for something, then walked back towards the building and away from the trash room.

Megan returned to her exploration. *It's just a rug. People throw out rugs all the time.* She sighed, pushing it back under the boxes. She turned to leave, putting all her weight onto a puddle on the slick floor. Frantically trying to steady herself, she slipped and fell back onto the object. Her left hand plunged into the now-exposed end of the wrapped carpet, and she caught sight of a reddish stain on the inside of her wrist. Meaghan stopped, slowly withdrawing her hand. She felt something sticky and wet coating her fingers. Trembling, she tugged her hand out.

Rushing to the small dirty sink in the corner, she scrubbed her hand raw with the small bits of cracked soap, trying to remove any trace of whatever this was. Her mind raced with what it could possibly be. *Blood, paint, cooking sauce. It has to be one of those*, she thought, allowing her mind to linger on blood.

She grabbed her recycling bag and scurried out of the room before anyone saw her.

*****

Riding the No1. Subway into Manhattan, she couldn't stifle a yawn.

"Rough night's sleep?" Her neighbor Zoe smiled at her.

When she'd first moved in, Meaghan had noticed Zoe exiting the building directly opposite her own each morning, walking down the steep stairs towards the subway, even stopping at the same coffee shop on the corner. After a week of shadowing each other, they bonded over the half and half.

"The neighbor above me seems to keep some strange work hours."

Too embarrassed to tell her about what had truly happened, Meaghan held her hand out in front of her to inspect it again for any trace. *Maybe it was paint, not blood, and maybe it was a dream,* she thought.

"Don't talk to me about neighbors. I have a family above me who bears more similarities to a gaze of Raccoons than to the human race." Zoe chuckled. "Hey, Earth to Meaghan. Are you

184

okay?"

Meghan realized her hand still hovered in the air. Dropping it quickly, she turned to Zoe and tried to focus.

"So, what's it going to be? Ghouls and Ghosts, Vampires and Zombies for your birthday party?" Zoe asked.

Meaghan stood to get ready for her stop. "Zombies have been done to death. Meet you at 28th Street station around six?" Zoe nodded and Meaghan stepped off the train.

A gentle rain greeted her as she pushed her way through the morning crowd of people, all vying for pole position in their struggle to get to work on time. Pulling open the glass doors of the Library where she worked, she made her way towards the back office. After rezoning the children's section today, she would browse through the horror section for some party inspiration and maybe a quick nap in the break room.

It was still raining when she met Zoe after work. Puddles formed on the pavements, creating a patchwork quilt of wet through which they tried their best to navigate. Deciding on an evil pumpkin theme, they bought enough strings of orange and black beads to decorate New Orleans. After drinks and the subway home, she couldn't wait to get to bed.

"Have a good sleep tonight. Don't let the neighbor stress you out." Zoe waved from across the street. As Meaghan waved back, she noticed a missing person's poster taped to the lamp post. Stopping quickly to read it, she felt an overwhelming sense of sadness. The girl was the same age as her.

***

Waiting for the elevator, she looked around at the tired 'Art Deco' foyer of the building, imagining it in 1939—pristine, admired by all who wandered through it. Now, patches of wallpaper peeled off to reveal the dirty plasterwork underneath and coupled with a musty smell nesting there.

When she finally got to her apartment, she sighed and pulled down the wall bed. She stopped every few minutes, listening for any noise from above. Convinced she just needed one good night's sleep, she snuggled under the covers with hope.

Waking in a cold sweat, pillows strewn on the floor, Meghan stared at the ceiling and breathed heavily. It wasn't the neighbor's boots this time; it had to be something else waking her. Rolling over to face the window, her ears picked up the sound and strained to hear it again.

Scratching. Long, deliberate scratching like an animal trying to claw its way out of a box. It came from directly above her, scratching the floor as though it wanted to get through to her side.

Meaghan put her hands over her ears. "Please go away, please go away," she chanted.

When she took her hands away, the sound remained—long scratches, one after the other after the other.

This is ludicrous, she thought, getting up and grabbing a sweater. She turned on the kitchen light and rummaged in the drawer for a flashlight. Grabbing it, she walked to the window and heaved it open. Then she crawled out onto the fire escape and made her way up one flight to the apartment above.

There was no light on and the curtains were drawn. Determined to find out what that noise was, she tugged on the window frame without thinking. It came as a surprise when the frame moved, and fueled by aggravation she kept pushing until the gap was wide enough for her

The Grim Keepers

body to fit through. She pulled the curtains gently to one side, then tapped the flashlight on the windowsill to get it to work; she flashed it slowly around the room. With no one home, she impulsively inched herself through the window on her stomach, falling onto the floor head first.

Meaghan froze in her crumpled state, then lifted the flash light and moved it around the room. It was barely furnished, with patchy wallpaper and a thick dust trying to find a home in her nose.

She pushed herself up to her feet and slinked along until she faced an old wardrobe door. Putting her ear to the door, she listened for the scratching—nothing. Trailing her fingers down the softness of the wood to the dirty patina of the lock, she couldn't believe the key had been left in the lock, almost egging her on to turn it.

She felt like she was invading the owner's privacy, but if there was something, or even someone, inside, she needed to know.

Holding the flashlight under her arm, her fingers paused on either side of the key. Breathing in, she quickly turned it, hearing the click of the lock before gently pulling the door towards her. It creaked open. Gripping the flashlight as a weapon, she took a step back, fearful of what might fall out. Stillness ensued; there was nothing in the wardrobe. It was empty.

Meaghan chastised herself. How obvious, to just look behind the first door with a key. Her eyes scanned the room, looking for another source of the annoying scratching sound. Suddenly, the elevator doors clanged open and heavy boots hit the hallway floor.

Meaghan heard them stop outside the apartment door, then heard a jangling of keys. Unsure what to do, she scrambled inside the wardrobe, pulling the door closed just in time. The front door opened and the heavy footfalls stomped towards her. Meaghan's stomach sat in knots as she tried not to make a sound. She could just see back into the room through slight cracks in the tired wood. The wardrobe's door was falling apart, like most things in this place.

The boots walked around the room before stopping right outside the wardrobe door. Meaghan's whole body shook with fear as she waited to be discovered. Then the footsteps walked away from her and towards the bathroom. Meaghan used her hands to feel around the floor of the wardrobe, noticing a loose side panel. She wanted to use her flash light to see what was there, but she knew she had to get out right then.

The Grim Keepers

She slowly exhaled, then sucked up as much courage as she needed, pushed open the cupboard door, and darted for the window. Cutting her hand on the rusty metal handrail as she pulled herself back through the window, she scurried down the fire escape as quickly as possible, unable to shake the feeling she'd just avoided something awful.

***

Her aching hand woke her the next morning, flashbacks of the previous evening infiltrating her brain. What was she thinking going up to that apartment? Whoever it was living there obviously never stayed the night. *Very strange.*

Meaghan spent most of her day shopping and preparing food for the party. She bought way more alcohol than everyone could drink, and used it to make up a huge punch bowl with orange coloring. It looked disgusting and tasted even worse. *Perfect*, she thought.

As the early evening approached, Meaghan got more exited for her party. She decided to make her way down to the rec room in the basement and add all the finishing touches. Pushing the elevator button, she waited and waited, eventually giving up to walk down the stairs.

Her evil pumpkin theme looked incredible;

the beads were hung and she had decorated the walls with cardboard pumpkins showing various sinister grins.

Dressed in her new outfit, she was ready for the fun to begin. She dimmed the lights low and lit candles ready to be placed inside the carved pumpkins each guest had been told to bring.

"Everything looks amazing," said Zoe when she arrived. "I've been carving my pumpkin all day! Does it look like me?" She laughed, holding it up in front of her.

"Not exactly, but nice try!"

"You still seem on edge. Is everything okay?"

"Yeah, I'm fine. Just a bit shaken up by the neighbor again. I'll fill you in later." Meaghan moved towards the door to welcome more guests. She was delighted with such a great turnout and loved that all her friends had made a great effort to dress up and join in the fun.

While dancing with Zoe, Meaghan noticed a blue hat slowly moving towards her. Straining her eyes to get a better look, she suddenly recognized it as the blue hat from the elevator. She couldn't believe he had come to her party.

"No, no, no," Meghan mumbled as she

moved around the room, looking for somewhere to hide.

"Meaghan?"

"Hi, yes. That's me. Nice to meet you. Do I know you?" Meagan squirmed in her own awkwardness. She felt like her discomfort was so obvious, but after a few cups of punch, she resigned herself to being able to blame it on the booze.

"I'm Alan. I live in the building. I found this bracelet outside my fire escape. It has Meaghan engraved on it, so when I heard your name mentioned outside I figured it must belong to you." Alan looked Meaghan directly in the eye and smiled sweetly as he handed the bracelet over.

"Wow, thanks. That's kind of you to go out of your way. I wonder how it got up there. Strange. Anyway, would you like to stay a moment, join in the fun?" Meaghan couldn't believe what her own words. She trembled inside from the realization he may have known she had gotten in to his apartment, and he was fearless in letting her know that he knew. Her mind danced with possibilities, none of them good, and yet she plastered on a fake innocence she could only hope he bought.

"Maybe another time. I have a few things I

have to do tonight. Have fun. Oh, and happy birthday."

Alan tipped his hat then walked out the door. Before she could move, Meaghan felt Zoe grab her arm, startling her. "OMG, who's the hunk?"

Meaghan looked at Zoe with nothing but disgust. "Zoe, that's my neighbor, the one making all the noise. I have a bad feeling about him. I'm serious."

"Oh, I have a bad feeling about him too. A very, very bad, deep, dark sensation... between my legs. If he was my neighbor, he could make all the noise he wanted. Hell, I'd help him make some noise if he let me!"

Zoe danced around in fits of giggles, and Meaghan felt helpless. She realized tonight was not the night she should be worrying about this, and resigned herself to having fun.

***

Meaghan woke with a huge pounding in her head. She still wore all her clothes and had been placed on her sofa in a drunken daze. She couldn't recall much from the night before, aside from realizing that making the punch was a terrible mistake. She was all alone, and it was now gone midday. *How long did I sleep?* she

193

wondered, making her way to the bathroom just in time to throw up half the contents of her stomach. She heard a groan from behind the shower curtain, revealing Ged from work, who had also lost half his stomach all over himself. His Frankenstein costume looked remarkably better now, but he was not a pretty sight. He must have been the person who brought her home. *Just as reliable out of work as in the office*, she mused.

She left him there and put a pair of large sweatpants and a t-shirt on the side of the tub so he could change when he woke up. Then she headed to the kitchen for a nice strong cup of coffee.

She had no idea where her phone was, and she sat staring into space as her mind fought to regain control.

"Hey," said Ged, rubbing his head as he stumbled in. "You got more coffee?"

"I sure do," she said with a giggle. "Thanks for bringing me home last night. I can't remember a thing. I must have been a real mess."

"You were pretty bad, but I made the mistake of drinking more of that deadly punch I found in the fridge while watching TV. That stuff is something else. I can't remember the last time I felt like this."

The Grim Keepers

"Did everyone get home okay?"

"Believe it or not, you were pretty much the last one standing. Your cute friend Zoe left with a guy I didn't recognize, and by the way she was hanging off him, I'm sure they had a good night."

"A guy? What guy? You knew everyone there."

"All I can tell you is he had a blue hat on. Other than that, it's anyone's guess. Shame though, I kinda like Zoe."

Meaghan rushed to the bathroom, emptying the rest of her stomach along with the thick black coffee. Her gut told her something was wrong. It was broad daylight and all her senses were going off. Still unable to think straight, she didn't know what to do. *Should I just go up and knock?*

She decided looking for her phone was a rational start, and she scoured the flat for her belongings. Frantically fingering the four-digit passcode, she was relieved to see no messages. She instantly called Zoe but the phone didn't answer, just rang and rang. At the same time, she heard a buzzing noise above her timed perfectly with the ringing. It sounded like a phone vibrating on the wooden floor. Then she heard the boots.

The Grim Keepers

Meaghan threw up everywhere, right in the middle of the living room. Ged rushed to her side, but she couldn't stop as fear overtook her body.

***

Mr. Fellows took a quick step back, trying to avoid the splash on his black, shiny brogues. A couple nurses rushed to Meaghan's side, supporting her body as she hurled in the center of the sterile room.

"Sorry about that, Mr. Fellows. Meaghan is a little unpredictable."

"What's wrong with her?" he asked firmly, unimpressed with the vomit now decorating his polished shoes.

"She's been with us for six months. She lives in an almost vegetative state, but she's functional. They found her in an apartment building, trussed up in a wardrobe. The neighbor alerted the authorities to strange goings on, and when they finally looked into it, they found her, barely alive. And they never caught the guy who did it. The doctors say she was so traumatized she just shut down. Tests show she's reliving a memory, over and over. Not necessarily what happened to her, but a sort of story, if you like. It usually ends with her being sick, unfortunately. Poor girl."

"Hmmm, nothing an increase in medication couldn't fix."

"That's not how we do things here Mr. Fellows. There's still a chance we can bring her back. These things take time."

"Indeed they do, but time usually involves money, and she won't be given the same care elsewhere."

"Is it decided, then? Stonewalls Institute of Psychiatric Medicine will be shut down?"

"Yes, I was hoping to see something here today to persuade me otherwise, but as it stands, my report will support the decision. I'd say it will take around four months to re-home everyone, but their needs will be met."

Both Nurse Baxter and Mr. Fellows looked over at Meaghan. She looked back at them in a wistful stare as her brain re-set and she snapped back into her never-ending story. Nurse Baxter mourned for the young woman every day, and vowed to help her find the best placement possible.

About Rachael Steele

Rachael is a novice writer and recently found solace in the craft whilst attempting to write chapters for a collaborative fiction novel. Her work was instantly admired for her creativity and research, pushing her to continue to pursue other avenues of writing. Rachael has recently been picked up by a travel website to work as their resident travel writer, and is excited to get stuck in.

Growing up in Australia, and traveling the world as a first class flight attendant, very little surprises her, yet everything fascinates her. You can connect with Rachael on Facebook.

https://www.facebook.com/rachael.gooch1

The Grim Keepers

The Dead Ringers
By Kevin Grover

Old Jefferson shoveled the last bit of dirt over the fresh grave, snorted, and spat. "You'll be on the graveyard shift," he said, turning to Zach. "It ain't a great job. You'll get tired as the night goes on, but you've got to remain alert. Listen out for 'em." He took a piece of string that ran down into the grave and tied it to a bell on a stake. "You hear the Dead Ringers, you'll need to act fast."

"I can handle it, Jeff," Zach told the older man. He was keen to make an impression, prove his worth. But he could see Jeff didn't trust him yet, thought he carried the reckless spirit of youth rather than the responsible attitude of the old. It didn't help that Jeff had been training Zach as his replacement, and after forty years in this graveyard he wasn't too keen to give it up. Looking around the jagged row of gravestones choked by weeds and chipped by the constant pecking of crows, Zach didn't understand why Jeff *didn't* want to walk away from it. Zach didn't have a choice: he needed the money. No one else wanted the Graveyard Shift with only the dead as company. It suited someone like Jeff who'd die on his own anyways. By the looks of him, it wouldn't be long.

"I know what you're thinking," Jeff continued. "Easy job, listening for the Dead Ringers. But you know how many graves you got here? There's three hundred at last count. This here makes it three hundred and one." He spat again on the mound of dirt. "So you're making your rounds at the dead of night and you hear the jingling of a bell from a Dead Ringer. Now you're running around, trying to locate where it's coming from out of over three hundred rotting corpses. And one of them out there is ringing that bell by the string tied to their wrist. As you make your way, tripping over gravestones, another bell starts ringing."

Zach shuddered. The sun had already sunken low on the horizon, bleeding red across the countryside. The church was a stone tower against the blood sun, sentinel to the dead. And across from the church was the little wooden shack, nestled in among the dead, looking ready to fall at the next gust of wind. That was Jeff's hut where the old fool put his feet up and slept through the night. Tonight it would be Zach's hut as he took on the town's tradition of the Graveyard Shift, a role born from superstition and an unfounded fear of the undead.

"Have the bells ever rung?" Zach asked, staring at a big black crow that settled on a gravestone, pecking at grubs. It chipped away at the brittle stone, looked over at him, and gave a cry, welcoming the coming night. They stared at each other, passing silent words. *You stay away from me, old crow, and I won't bother you.* A mist crawled across the ground, swirled around the graves, and Zach resigned himself to a long, cold night.

"When I was a younger man, probably about your age, I first heard the Dead Ringers. I was like you, taking a job on from a man I thought was an old fool. The dead are dead, thought I, they didn't need a string tied to their wrists to ring a bell as they lay in peace within their coffin. Weren't gonna suddenly come to life and try to rise. But I'll never forget the night I heard the Dead Ringers. Every bell in the graveyard went and I ain't ever been so scared as that night."

Zach stared at Jeff, trying to see the lie in his eyes. *Hoping* to see a lie. "W-what happened? The dead all woke up at once?" Generations of his family were buried in the graveyard, sleeping right under his feet. His own mother lay there and he shuddered at the thought that she might one day ring a bell just for her son.

Jeff grunted. "I grabbed my gun from the shack, though my hands were shaking real bad. Didn't think I'd shoot straight if I got a dead 'un come at me. It was pitch black out there and all I had was a lantern and the light of a full moon to see by. The air was filled by the ringing bells, but I stood firm, stayed at the gate to the graveyard and waited."

"And?"

"Bells went silent. I guess it was the dead playing with me on my first night. They like to scare the living, play games with them. Stand firm against them, boy. Since then, I never slept on the graveyard shift, always a hand on my gun." He knelt down by the freshly planted bell, tested for a tight knot, and gave the bell a couple of rings. It clanged through the darkening graveyard, giving a voice to the dead. The crow cried in response, spread its wings, and flew up into a gnarled old tree twisting into the sky. The sun was almost gone, the final light of day clinging to the horizon.

Jeff straightened up, pulled his coat around himself for warmth, and headed for the gate. Zach followed him in silence, wondering what he'd got himself into. Wasn't like he was smart enough to do anything else. He wasn't cut out for farming like his dad wanted. He'd laughed when he heard Jefferson was getting too old to watch the dead, joked that he should take it on. The pay was good. You mainly worked from sunset to sunrise, helping tie the strings joining the dead to the bells and digging a grave when needed. The joke turned serious as he thought it over. Grab a few hours' sleep in the morning and he'd have the day to do what he liked. Even catch a sleep in Jeff's hut. The dead just wanted to sleep. But as the dark came and the cold set in, Zach had his first second thought.

When they got to the rusty iron gate, Jeff pulled out a set of metal keys on a hoop. He went over each key, but Zach was only half listening. "This here's the gate. This the church front door and the back door, here. Little key the hut."

Zach took the keys. But he was looking

across the graveyard, watching the stones for movement, seeing shadows against the church. An owl hooted and a bat flew overhead. The crow cried out again and there was the sound of beak on stone, chipping away. A wind whipped up around them, chilling Zach. "Won't the wind make the bells ring?"

Jeff gave a short laugh, spat over his shoulder. "Only thing ringing those bells are the Dead Ringers. Remember, if you hear the bells, you better be ready. The dead come back feral things, wanting nothing more than to feast on the living. You gotta be quick and you gotta be a good shot. Aim for the head, right between the eyes if you can. One more thing, make sure you never walk around the church Widdershins. That's anticlockwise. If it don't summon the dead, you'll call the devil for sure." He sniffed the air. "Gonna be a cold night. Plays a good 'un, the cold, with my arthritis." He turned to go, paused, added, "There's a hip flask of whiskey in the hut, keep you warm. Don't go swigging too much and fall asleep. Don't want the dead creeping up on you. Keep your eyes on the bells." Nodding a farewell, old Jefferson left the dead to Zach, his final graveyard shift done. He walked with the stiff steps of age and finality.

The Grim Keepers

Locking the gate, Zach made a first patrol around the graveyard, keeping to the crumbling stone wall, fearing he'd walk over a grave and wake the dead. On Jeff's advice, he made sure he walked clockwise around the yard. His eyes scanned the still bells, the string pulled tight, ready for the slight movement to ring the bell as the dead woke. The strings hung like umbilical cords, linking the dead in their wooden wombs as they waited for birth. Whistling, he broke the silence tickling at his sanity.

There was no one around, the town two miles down the old country lane. The church sat on top of a hill, looking over the town as it slept through the night as it had done for decades, well before his granddad's time. And in those distant days, it had been a last stand against the walking dead, the villagers barricading themselves inside as the dead tried to smash their way in. It had happened in his great-great-grandfather's time, long enough ago to have faded into a passed-down tale through the generations. Kids would scare each other about it, how Hobb Village had been overrun by the undead. And people believed it enough to have a graveyard shift, a guardian to watch over the dead and make sure they remained that way.

The Grim Keepers

Superstitions and old traditions—there was no truth in any of it. Just like Jeff's story about the bells ringing, it was a lie designed to scare and entertain on dark winter nights when you huddled around the fire and the darkness pressed against your windows. You'd go to bed that night with a sense of unease, a fear of the night as you stared from your bedroom window and the wind howled. He wanted his bed right now, felt tired already before it was even full dark.

It took him ten minutes to walk the entire graveyard at a brisk pace, and he ended his patrol at Jeff's hut. The hut had a rusted metal roof with a wonky chimney, a single window looking east where the rising sun would shine through and signal the end of the graveyard shift. Opening the door, he went inside, smelling old wood and a hint of tobacco from Jeff's pipe. A single lantern hung from the roof and Zach hunted around on the table in the dark for some matches. He found them, struck one, and lit the lantern. It spluttered out a faint glow, sending shadows dancing around the hut. He sat down on a chair, swung his feet up on the desk, and watched the fog growing thicker, pressing up to the window. Only a thin pane of glass existed between him and the night. He didn't like it, didn't trust the night would be kept out there with the dead.

Every bell in the graveyard went and I ain't ever been so scared as that night.

Searching through a cabinet, Zach found Jeff's hip flask. He shook it and the contents sloshed around inside. Felt nearly full. Must've filled it as a welcome to the new job. He took a swig and the whiskey burned a path into his stomach, scattering the chills. Another few sips and he settled back in the chair.

It was soon full dark outside and the fog hung thick against the window, desperate to come inside. The dead continued to sleep, and a bird landed on the metal roof, pecking at it. Zach welcomed the sound, hating the deathly silence of the graveyard. He had never been up here so late, was shocked by how dark it was.

The lantern flickered, threatening to go out, and the primal fear of dark took him. But the light was stubborn and kept alight. It shone on Jeff's shotgun, a box of cartridges spilling across the table. Zach had fired a gun before, hunting rabbits with his dad, knew he could handle it if needed. But what if his mum rung her bell, came creeping through the fog to the spluttering light at the hut? Could he shoot her rotten corpse, send her back to the ground?

The Grim Keepers

As the whiskey warmed him, he felt his eyes growing heavy, snapped them open and struggled against sleep. The bird on the roof had stopped pecking at the metal, now scratching around up there, tiny feet like raindrops on tin. He thought of tiny fingers tapping to be let in, imagined the dead up there on the roof and shivered. Another swig from the flask and it soothed him towards sleep, encouraged him into the land of dreams. He drifted into a light doze.

When he woke up, the lantern had gone out and complete darkness surrounded him. He searched blindly for the box of matches, desperate for the light to return. His hands shook, knocking over unseen objects in his haste. Outside, an owl hooted. Finally he found the box, struck a match, and held it to the lantern.

A face stared in at him through the window. The match burned his fingers and he dropped it. Hands shaking, he struck another and it lit up the window again. There was no one there, just his own pale reflection looking back at him. He lit the lantern, felt comforted by the weak light it cast. He was jumping at reflections, thinking they were something else.

The dead.

Zach loaded the gun, just in case. There

was a lot of silver in the church and he had to remember the very real threat of thieves. Not that locals came to the church at night, fearing the sound of the Dead Ringers. And if he'd seen someone out there, he'd better go check. How would it look if the church got burgled on his first night? His dad would tell him he wasn't cut out for the job. Jeff would agree with him, wonder what he was thinking letting a youngster take over such an important job. Unhooking the lantern, Zach pushed the door open and stepped out into the fog, feeling the air freeze his face. He could just make out the gravestones sticking up like rotten teeth in a mouth full of gaps.

He walked around the church, looking for the flicker of a lantern within, but saw nothing. He checked the door, walked around to the back, and checked that, too. It was secure. Pulling out his pocket watch, he checked the time in the weak light of the lantern. It was just coming to midnight and he felt a shuddering cold ripple through him. He jumped as another owl hooted. Something fluttered by in front of his face. Probably a bat. Walking from the church, he'd forgotten if he'd walked clockwise or anticlockwise.

Widdershins....If it don't summon the dead, you'll call the devil for sure.

The Grim Keepers

It was too cold for this, too dark. He made his way back to the hut, careful where he stepped.

Then came the ringing of a bell, somewhere in the graveyard. It gave two big rings and fell silent. Had he imagined that? It rang again, sending his heart racing. Kids had to be playing in the graveyard. Or Jeff had snuck back to see if Zach was sleeping on the job.

He wandered in the direction he'd heard the bell, moving carefully between the stones with his lantern held high. The bell rang again, echoing through the cold night air. Had mum come ringing, calling to her son?

"Who's there?" he called out, trying to sound as if he wasn't scared. Truth was, he was terrified, ready to run screaming into the night and back to town. He realized he'd left the gun back in the hut. He considered going back for it when the bell rang again, just a few feet away. It didn't stop, one-second gaps between each peal. Zach remained still, trying to look through a mix of fog and night. Something moved in the corner of his eye. Spinning round, he dropped the lantern. It went out and plunged him into darkness with nothing but the ringing of the bell to keep him company. A whimper escaped his lips and he stumbled back. He tripped on a stone, fell on his

212

back into the cold earth, and tensed. Something walked towards him, dragging feet across the ground. A groan drifted through the fog and he scrabbled away from it.

The bell continued to ring.

Zach jumped to his feet, ran blind through the night. He came to the hut, pulled the door open, and slammed it shut behind him. He leaned against the flimsy door, tendrils of fog curling under and around it. Grabbing the gun, he gripped it close to his chest. More bells rang one after the other around the graveyard, sounding deep within his mind, challenging his sanity on the verge of snapping. There were three hundred and one bodies buried out there, every one of them a Dead Ringer. The ringing triggered a sudden manic hysteria within Zach and he laughed over the sound. The crow returned to the roof, pecking at the tin and adding to the orchestra of madness.

I guess it was the dead playing with me on my first night. They like to scare the living, play games with them.

The bells went suddenly silent and the only sound was the rattling of the window from a relentless wind. The crow gave a cry, as though calling the dead back to action. Peering out the window, all Zach saw were the crooked graves through the fog. The howl of the wind gave the graves the sound of sadness, entrancing Zach with what he thought of as the song of the dead. Not a soul moved out there and he relaxed, the tension passing from his body with a shuddering sigh.

Then he saw them, figures in the fog among the graves. They came towards the hut, silently stalking him. Their unnaturally twisted bodies moved with the slow stiffness of death. As they walked, he heard the bells, chiming towards his death.

The door swung open in the wind and Zach slammed it closed, fumbling with his keys to lock it. He dropped them in his panic, couldn't see where they went. Nails scratched at the wood and Zach pushed his body up against the door as the dead slammed into it. Gaunt, lifeless faces with sunken black eyes pressed up to the window and stared in at him. The walls splintered around him and arms burst through the frail wood, hands pawing at him. Strings were tied to their wrists and the bells rang at their feet as they fell onto Zach. His screams drowned out the ringing of the bells. Teeth sank into his flesh and he tensed as hot pain ripped into him.

A gunshot fired into the night and the dead looked up from their prey. Another shot went off, deafening Zach. The closest Dead Ringer fell back, head exploding in a spray of black gunk that splashed over Zach's face. The dead rose, stumbled away into the fog, but the bullets hunted them, brought them down in piles. Zach sat up, hugging his knees to his chest, and watched as a figure strolled through the graveyard, rounding the Dead Ringers up with blasts from the gun. The figure knelt down beside Zach, studying him with a grizzled face.

"Did they bite you?" Jefferson asked, eyes narrowing. He looked up into the fog. "Walked the church widdershins, did you? Now, what are we going to do with you? Can't have you walking about, can we? Got to bury you, for your family's sake. I'd burn you if I had my way."

Zach tried to speak but coughed up blood instead. His body felt like it was on fire, spreading from the bites of the Dead Ringers. His head spun, vision growing dark. Time seemed to make a few jumps and he found himself dragged by the feet through the dirt. Another jump in time and he felt cold gripping his body. When he tried to move, he found a paralysis had taken him. Jeff pulled Zach's arm up, tied a string to his wrist. The sun was rising, chasing the night and the fog away. Jeff pulled the string tight and it dug into Zach's skin.

"I hope you never have to ring that bell," Jeff said, lowering the coffin lid onto him. He threaded the string through a hole and as Zach felt his life fade, he realized where the string would be tied. In the darkness of his new womb, he heard Jeff testing the bell. *His bell.*

It gave two rings and fell silent. Zach felt himself falling into the sleep of death, unable to find the strength to ring the bell himself. Not quite yet.

Kevin Grover - Kent, UK

Kevin is a horror writer who lives in Kent, England. Kevin's biggest influence is Stephen King. Kevin has been writing from a young age and describes himself as the ultimate geek. When not writing, you can often find him watching old episodes of Doctor Who. He has been previously published in 'Writing Magazine' in the UK, having come runner up in their 2012 ghost story competition with *Pack Up Your Troubles*, a story about a wartime ghost come back to visit his wife.

Father's Song is his first novel and takes the reader on a journey into the dark origins of nursery rhymes. It has recently been published and is now available through Amazon. You can connect with Kevin using the following links:

Website: www.kevingrover.co.uk
Facebook: www.facebook.com/Kevin.grover
Twitter: @groverkevin

The Grim Keepers

The Man in the Black Hat
By Alex Benitez

All was well in the small town of Fernwood. It was only ten years after the long string of child abductions, but those incidents had almost been forgotten. A total of eleven small children had seemingly vanished from playgrounds, or on their way home from school, without a shred of evidence to assist authorities in finding them. The police had relied on the media for help to track down the perpetrators, but not a single soul could offer any clues. The cases had gone colder than a winter's night, but a fleet of people knew who was responsible. Eleven children had disappeared in only a few months' time, but the new generation of children were wiser.

The Grim Keepers

If you were to ask any child in Fernwood who did it, they'd say *the man in the black hat* without hesitation. They saw him on the edge of playgrounds, standing across the street from the elementary school, anywhere children gathered. No adult noticed the man in the black hat, and only laughed his name off as modern folklore. To them, the man in the black hat was a superstitious myth conjured up by the kids of Fernwood, but the children knew better. They knew the man's rules and they had no sympathy for those who didn't follow them. By word of mouth alone, the kids of Fernwood learned to coexist with the man in the black hat, but sadly, not every child knew.

Summer had nearly ended and Michael Drake's mother wished nothing more than for her son to make some friends before the school year started. She had just accepted a decent job near the quaint little town, so they'd moved, but uprooting their lives proved difficult for Michael. His mom hoped the transition would go smoother if he had a few friends before his first day in a strange new school, so she decided to take him to Fernwood Park for the day.

The park was a vast field housing three baseball diamonds, a soccer field, a basketball court, and various small playgrounds for the enjoyment of the neighborhood kids.

Michael's exhausted mother sat in the bleachers beside a baseball diamond and sighed. "Okay Michael, go play."

"I don't wanna!" Michael immaturely protested.

"Go!" she aggressively, and pulled out a folded Vanity Fair magazine from her purse. "It's not normal for little boys to be around their mothers all day."

"Fine," he moaned as he left to find his way through the large park.

He tried to play tetherball, swing on the swings, and use the seesaw, but the activities proved less than exciting all alone. The other kids were not willing to include a new, different face, so Michael ended up sitting by himself at the top of the big slide. He just sat there a while, leaning his chin on his hands, feeling sad and left out.

Suddenly, Michael heard a voice from the ground below him. "Hey, you!"

Michael looked down and saw another boy standing there with a big red ball. "Who, me?" he asked the boy.

"Yeah! I wanna start a dodgeball game. Wanna play?"

Michael's face brightened. "Sure." He then

slid down the slide to join his new companion.

"Okay, let's go," the other boy said, and they scouted the park for other players.

"I'm Michael."

"Greg," the boy said as he eyed down the other kids.

"Do people here usually play dodgeball?"

"No."

As they searched for additional players, Michael saw him. A scrawny, hunched-over old man in a black hat with a long face. It was a dark, dirty, pork-pie hat, worn above a disheveled suit like any common tramp, but the eerie thing about the man was his face. He only had black, gaping holes for eyes and a mouth, leading to a place where a spirit was supposed to be. He just stood there at the edge of the park by the woods, staring at the kids.

"Who's that?" Michael asked.

Greg quickly dropped his ball and forcibly shifted Michael's body so that his back faced the man in the black hat. "Never look at him! Never ever!" he whispered.

"What? Why?"

"If you don't look at him, he can't get you," Greg explained.

"What do you mean?"

The Grim Keepers

"It happened last year. Have you heard of Audrey Dalton?"

"No."

"I know because it was Mrs. Dalton's daughter," Greg continued. "I had her in third grade. She said she was sick of him and was going to tell him to go away and leave us all alone. We told her not to, but she said she wasn't scared. When she went to talk to him, he took her. It was all over the TV and they put her picture up everywhere. Mrs. Dalton left school and I heard she's really, really sad. Just don't look at him. It's better that way."

"Yeah," Michael agreed, and realized the story made him shake a little.

"Look, I'm gonna go to the jungle gym until he goes away. You can come if you want."

"Okay," Michael said before Greg hastily picked up his ball and ran to the jungle gym.

Michael followed Greg, but he could feel the man in the black hat's cold, horrid gaze coating his back. His neck slowly turned until he saw the man in the corner of his eye. Michael noted he still put more and more distance between himself and the man. How could he 'get him' if the man didn't move from that spot? Curiosity eventually got the better of him, and Michael decided to take

223

one last, good look.

He turned around, still walking backwards to create more of a gap between himself and the creepy man in the hat. He'd predicted correctly; the man hadn't moved at all. A slight relief came over his body as he got his eye-full without incident, and he contently turned back around.

Then he bumped into something, and looked up to see that he'd run straight into the very same man in the black hat. The man placed his withered, crinkled fingers on Michael's shoulders and the boy froze in his tracks. The man in the black hat leaned down until he was face to face with Michael. The boy peered deep into the endless dark voids of his face, and a terrifying sound rang out. It sounded like a reverse shriek that Michael was certain only he could hear. He stood there among the other children of Fernwood, but he knew he was trapped. Michael felt himself being sucked away.

Sometime later, Mrs. Drake finished her magazine and looked up at the playing children. She scanned the scene for a few minutes, trying to locate her son, but he was nowhere to be seen. Keeping alarm at bay, she calmly combed through the park for Michael. When she realized she had covered most of the park, her worries formed into full-fledge panic.

"Michael!" she shouted out at groups of children. "Michael! Michael!" She called out to every corner of the playground. Frantic now, she dashed to a little boy holding a red ball who was trying to start a dodgeball game. "Excuse me! Little boy."

"Yes?" Greg said.

"Have you seen a boy named Michael? This tall? Brown hair?"

"Oh," Greg uttered as his face darkened into a cold shroud. "I told him not to look at the man, but he did it anyway. I'm sorry. He's gone."

She backed away from the boy, chilled to the marrow by his reply. As she gained her composure, she headed back to the park calling her son's name over and over.

Mrs. Drake searched hysterically for her son at Fernwood Park all that day, and all the while the man in the black hat remained. He just stood there, at the edge of the park by the woods, staring at the kids.

About Alex Benitez

Alex Benitez is a thirty-year-old author who has been writing seriously for the last five years. Alex considers himself a storyteller and has been developing stories since his infancy. Alex had no actual formal training in writing when he wrote his first novel 'Rose Star Runners', and continues to write, picking up tricks of the trade as he goes along. Alex has a day job at a trendy Mexican restaurant and saves what he can for future publications. His future projects include a Horror/Thriller novel called 'High Tower Black', four more installments of the 'Rose Star Runners' series, and an untitled comic he will submit to *Heavy Metal Magazine*.

The Grim Keepers

The Open Door
By Crystal M M Burton

There are many misconceptions about the world beyond the mirror. The most popular is the belief that it is the opposite of our own—literally a 'mirror image' of our world. Left becomes right, true becomes false, and we spend hours of our lives staring in wonder, imagining what life would be like if a few aspects of it were backwards. The idea of such a world is a mostly pleasant one.

This is wrong.

The world in the mirror is actually an impression of ours. It is a living absorption of our thoughts and emotions. It makes no distinction between lies and truth. It only understands the intensity behind our notions and perceptions, and the depth of faith we stock into our words.

We have always had windows into this

mysterious realm. Witches and warlocks of the old religion were said to have passed objects through reflections in water and glass. It was only recently, in the 1800s, that a German chemist by the name of Justus von Liebig found a way to create a door. With the invention of the mirror, the concept of travel between worlds became a dangerous reality.

***

Callie Ashegrove was all too familiar with her reflection.

It was always there—in the spotless window of her brand new car, in the crystal-clear surface of her in-ground pool, and in every bright, taunting mirror. It constantly showed her things she couldn't change. Like her nose being too big for her face. Or her eyes being unnaturally far apart. The mirror mocked her and ridiculed her, but she thrived on the sadistic delusions her mind perceived. She was obsessed both with her image and how people viewed her.

Her story begins on a chilly October morning. She was only in her second month at the community college, but she knew her growing popularity was largely based on her beauty, which she perfected each day before going out into the world. She brushed the thick curls of her long blonde hair, smoothing them into perfect waves of gold. She scrupulously applied her makeup, paying extra attention to the framing of her sea-green eyes. She paused for a second too long to check her reflection. As usual, the longer she scrutinized her appearance, the more flaws she observed.

"Ugh. Look at those pores. No amount of foundation can cover those," she said, disgusted. Her reflected self seemed to be offended as well, and the frown on her face created harsh lines that only increased her aversion. She took a step back and affected a smile, trying to convince herself she was fine, as long as no one looked too closely. As she debated whether or not to put on a second layer of makeup, her phone beeped. It was Andrea, her best friend since middle school, asking for a ride. Callie texted back saying she was on her way, then stole one last glance at the mirror before heading out the door.

*** Ten Days to Halloween ***

She walked back to her silver Prius that afternoon when she spotted him across the parking lot. Fox Warren—the smart, funny, handsome Quarterback, and the only reason she had ever gone to football games.

"Hey, Fox," she said, greeting him with a smile. "How was practice?"

"It was pretty good. Jefferson's finally getting that spiral down. We might actually win a few games this year."

"Finally! I don't know how he ever made the team."

"I do. Daddy's got money."

They gossiped as they walked right past her car, instead ending up three rows over next to his Camaro. He climbed inside the driver's seat and turned sideways to face her. She twirled the ends of her hair, directly in front of her plunging neckline, hoping the movement would compel him to notice her chest. As always, his eyes were drawn downward. He trailed off mid-sentence, biting his lower lip. A car horn nearby interrupted his fantasizing, and he picked back up where his sentence left off.

"So, anyways, I was saying I hear some chick from Physics is throwing a party next Saturday, a big Halloween scare-fest. Guess who's going with me? Now, costumes are encouraged, and you *will* be wearing one." He narrowed his eyes and waved a finger at her, mimicking a serious tone. "So I want to see that sexy nurse outfit you wore for my birthday." He ended with a wink, and she rolled her eyes as her face flushed.

"Um, that was actually a private showing," she teased. "But yeah, I'll totally be there."

"Great! Well, I'm off. Catch ya later, gorgeous." He revved the engine, blew her a kiss, and took off. Callie was left standing there in the parking lot, watching his flashy red car drive away.

"I guess I need to lose five pounds by next weekend," she said aloud.

"Wow," a voice answered from behind her. Callie turned to see Andrea walking over, shaking her head lightly with an amused grin. "Just wow. He has you wrapped so far around his penis, it's a wonder you aren't pregnant."

"Oh, shut it," Callie retorted. "He's Fox Warren. He has every girl on campus wrapped around that thing. I'm just the only one who actually gets it."

"For now. His eyes like to wander."

Callie let out an exasperated sigh. She wished Andrea wasn't always so brutally honest, or so willing to share her opinions.

*** Six Days to Halloween ***

Callie sat in the passenger seat of Fox's

speeding Camaro as they cruised along the highway. He had the windows down and his favorite rock station blaring. Callie's hair whipped in the wind, lashing at her face. She knew it was not a sexy look. She pulled her hair back into a messy ponytail, then reached for the purple compact mirror and eyeliner pencil she kept in her purse. She balanced the mirror in the palm of her hand and touched up the dark lines encircling her eyes.

Without warning, Fox cursed and slammed on the brakes. Callie's mirror went flying out of her hand, collided with the dashboard, then bounced to the floor and landed at her feet.

"Son of a bitch—did you see that jerk cut me off?" Fox growled. He held one hand out the window, directing a middle finger at the offending driver while honking the horn with the other. He muttered a few more expletives before eventually glancing at Callie. She was bent over, grasping for her mirror. Her fingers folded around the plastic exterior and she sat up straight, brushing a few stray hairs out of her eyes.

"Hey, you might want to fix that." Fox chuckled, pointing to her cheek.

Worried, Callie looked into her mirror to see what he meant. "Shit," she cursed.

The Grim Keepers

"I know. Looks like you missed," Fox teased, laughing at the line of black trailing from the corner of her eye over to her left ear.

"No, not that. My mirror's busted." Callie stared, disappointed, at the long, thin cracks spread across the circular glass. It seemed the initial hit was directly in the center, just about where her nose appeared in her reflection. From there, a thin line curved upward to the right, spreading out in a spiderweb pattern as it reached the edge of the glass. "Damn. This is my favorite mirror, too."

"It's all right, babe. That was my bad. I'll get you a new one."

It took Callie ten minutes to fix her makeup. She wasn't completely satisfied with it, but she figured it was good enough. She looked over at Fox to ask his opinion, closing her mirror in the process. When she turned her head to the left, she didn't see that her reflection still stared straight at her.

*** Five Days to Halloween ***

Callie exhaled contentedly as she dipped her head beneath the water. Cheer practice really worn her out that afternoon, and the hot bath eased her aching muscles. She could feel the heat permeating to her core, and the softness of the water relaxed her.

She lay there in the tub, trying to clear her mind. She didn't want to think about Fox, or Andrea's advice that he wasn't right for her, or her Chemistry project due in two weeks, and she certainly didn't want to think about the party. She was pretty sure Melinda would be there, and she couldn't stand her; Melinda always had that homewrecker look in her eyes when she flirted with Fox, and a repulsively smug grin whenever he smiled at her. Knowing Melinda, she'd wear her bikini to the party, and 'accidentally' lose her top. If she did, Callie would have no reservations about ripping that top into strips and shoving it down the girl's throat.

Sighing, Callie gave up trying to relax her mind; it wasn't working. She reluctantly pulled the plug from the drain and stood. Wrapping a large towel around her body and a smaller one around her hair, she stepped in front of the mirror, burying her toes in the thick, soft bath rug. She went about her evening routine at the sink: gently exfoliating with her favorite Brown Sugar and Vanilla face wash, brushing her teeth, and giving her hair a vigorous rub down with the small towel.

The Grim Keepers

Once satisfied that the basics were taken care of, she wiped a streak of fog away from the glass so she could see. She examined her appearance, hating how round her face looked when her hair was wet. Pulling her hair back tightly, she shook her head in disgust.

"I look like a guy," she whispered. She tilted her chin down to get a new angle. "Hmph. An ugly guy." She scrutinized her image until she found something on which to focus.

"Oh, hell no," she told her reflection as she picked up her tweezers. "That's got to go, right now."

She quietly hummed to herself as she set to work. One by one, she plucked tiny black hairs from around her eyebrows, ensuring they kept their perfect, curving shape. She paused to admire her handiwork, running her index fingers along both eyebrows. Just beneath her focus, she saw herself wink.

She took a step back. She hadn't winked. She squeezed her eyes shut for a moment, then locked her gaze with her own reflection and concentrated. Just as she was about to stop her seemingly pointless staring contest, the reflection slowly—deliberately—winked again. This time Callie flung the bathroom door open and rushed

237

out into the hallway, stopping to lean against her bedroom doorframe. Her paranoia was getting the best of her. She assumed she was more tired than she felt, and without even blow-drying her hair— let alone getting dressed—she lay down in bed, buried herself beneath her thick comforter, and went straight to sleep.

*** Four Days to Halloween ***

Tuesday morning came and went. Callie had completely forgotten about the strange incident from the night before, and now sat with Andrea at their favorite Chinese restaurant, waiting to be served.

"So, I saw Melinda this morning," Andrea told her. "She was bragging to some people in the hallway, probably to anyone who would listen, saying she just got a new costume for Saturday. A nurse outfit."

Callie slammed her hands down on the table. "Dammit! Seriously?" she growled. "Of course she did. How does she even know? Did she raid my closet or something?"

"I'm sure Fox told her."

"Andrea, please try to be on my side on this," Callie begged her friend. "I do like this guy.

238

Even with his jerk moments." Andrea pursed her lips and looked thoughtfully at Callie.

"Okay, maybe he told one of the guys on the field and she heard about it. Guys like to brag, right?"

"Thank you."

"Uh huh."

Their food hadn't arrived yet, so Callie went to the bathroom. As she slid open the lock on the stall, she realized she could hear the faint echo of a woman singing. It was so soft she wasn't sure she really heard it at first. The words were inaudible, but the eerie melody still gave her chills. She stood there with her hand on the open stall door, straining to hear the mysterious music. The voice sounded so familiar, but Callie couldn't quite place it.

She shrugged it off and went to the sink to wash her hands. The mirrors here were a cheaply made imitation with a reflective metal surface. They were dented and dinged up, grossly distorting the image. Callie didn't even bother looking into them, because she knew it would only aggravate her. The running water muffled the singing, which had gotten slightly louder. Off and on, she was almost certain she could hear crying, but it wasn't distinguishable enough to tell for

239

sure.

Back at the table, she asked Andrea if she had heard any music, but wasn't surprised when her friend said she hadn't. Callie tucked away her curiosity as she looked around to admire the décor. She did this every time they ate here. She loved the tiny red paper lanterns strewn around the edge of the room, and the large, gilded mirrors mounted beside each hanging lamp, reflecting bright, golden light around the room. She especially loved the mirrors; they were overlaid with beautiful images and Chinese writings. The one hanging at their favorite booth depicted a lovely woman in bright yellow Hanfu, her face painted white and her lips dyed blood-red, dancing with serpentine dragons in front of a wide, flourishing water garden. Callie always envied that woman; she was beautiful and talented and had the strength of dragons to see her through her troubles.

As she oggled the mirror, the low, sultry singing once again drifted through the air. It was the loudest she had heard it so far, yet just barely above a whisper. Andrea still denied hearing anything. Callie tilted her head, intent on discovering the source of the haunting melody. It seemed to get louder as she got closer to the wall.

The Grim Keepers

She settled into the idea that it came from the other side of the wall, and with the mystery solved, turned her attention back to Andrea and the food that had just been set on the table.

At home a few hours later, Callie hummed to herself as she washed dishes, repeating the melody she had heard at the restaurant. She made a mental note to look for the song later; having a song stuck in her head was ten times worse when she didn't know any of the words. She had just finished up and dried her hands on the kitchen towel when the song she hummed suddenly became a duet.

She froze. The tune continued, and Callie's mind went blank. Her first coherent thought was that the words still sounded muffled. When she finally recovered from the initial shock, she went into overdrive, searching the house for clues; she was determined to find either the singer or a music player. She even considered that perhaps she had accidentally picked up someone else's cell phone and the mysterious singing was actually a ringtone.

When she wandered into the hall, she was confused. The sound seemed to come from both the bathroom and the bedroom. Choosing to begin with the bathroom, she crossed the threshold and came face to face with herself.

The girl in the mirror was no longer a simple reflection. She was the mysterious singer, repeating the ominous melody that had so captivated Callie. Only the reflection's face moved independently; Callie waved her arms over her head and spun in a circle, and her image followed every motion save for her expression. Her reflection continued singing, and Callie could finally understand the words.

> Save me from my hate
> Protect me from my fate
> Deliver me from here
> One day each year

"How are you doing that?" Callie whispered. She had her back pressed up against the wall opposite the mirror and her eyes never strayed from her reflection. The look on her mirrored face showed wistful sorrow, and with each repetition of the supernatural chant a tear fell from her glassy eyes. Callie raised a hand to her own face, her cheeks feeling the hot sting of the tears, but she pulled her hand away dry. "This isn't possible..." She tore her gaping eyes away from the mirror and ran out of the bathroom and into her bedroom. The reflection followed her there as well, this time presenting itself in the full-length cheval mirror standing beside her dresser.

Standing face to face with herself once more, Callie gathered up the courage to reach out her hand. She lightly grazed the surface of the mirror, relieved to feel the cold glass against her fingertips.

"Who are you?" Callie uttered.

Her reflection didn't answer. She only offered a sad smile and continued her melodic chorus.

Callie slept in the living room that night with her headphones turned up as loud as they would go. Though they drowned out the sound of her reflection, they couldn't erase the song from her mind.

*** Three Days to Halloween ***

Andrea didn't believe her. Fox had been busy the past few days, and while she was all alone, Calli was going out of her mind.

She had tried to show Andrea her reflection and its eerie song, but when Andrea looked into the mirror, she didn't see anything out of place.

The Grim Keepers

"Are you feeling all right?" she had asked. "I know you've been stressed lately, but if you're having a mental breakdown, this might not be the best time to be partying and stuff. You know, with people that might aggravate your...condition."

"I'm serious! You really don't see it?" Callie had tried, but Andrea didn't believe in what she couldn't see. Or hear. She truly felt as if she were going crazy. Andrea had gone to school and Callie was left by herself, missing class and losing her sanity. She stood up, pulled herself together as best she could, and stalked into the bedroom to confront whatever mental illness harassed her through the looking glass.

"What do you want from me? Why am I seeing you?" Callie shouted at the unusually still image. For the first time, the reflection spoke rather than sang.

"I'm a reflection. You will always see me." Callie felt a wave of nausea coming on. She leaned against the edge of her bed to steel herself, then addressed the mirror again, lowering her voice to a normal tone.

"That's just it, though. You're a reflection. You shouldn't be talking on your own. Oh, God, if anyone saw me right now, I bet they'd think I'm going mental." Callie put a hand to her forehead, checking for fever. Though she didn't feel hot, her nausea threatened to make her collapse. She swallowed hard, fighting back the urge to empty the contents of her lunch all over the floor. She eased onto her mattress, praying that the simple act of sitting down would help to quell her churning stomach. Luckily, it did. When she eventually spoke again, she realized that her reflection was still standing.

"You can move on your own, now," Callie stated. Her reflection only nodded. "I still don't understand why."

"You unlocked the door," the girl in the mirror whispered.

Callie stared, waiting for a deeper explanation. Her reflection looked down, as if composing herself. When she raised her face once more, Callie was shocked by the honesty of her somber smile. It was as if her image could actually feel emotion. It was almost too much for Callie to bear—the idea that an image on a piece of glass could feel anguish, loss, hope, all of which Callie saw reflected back at her in her own eyes. Tears crept down both Callie's cheeks and those of her image, and Callie had to feel her face again to be sure the tears were her own this time.

"You unlocked the door," her reflection

repeated, hope glistening in her fragile words. "You can save me. You can protect me. You can open the door."

"What door?" Callie asked with trepidation. The girl stepped forward, and for a moment Callie thought she was going to collide with the clear wall standing between them.

The reflection stopped at the frame and put her hands up on the thick glass. "This door," she said softly.

The conversation only left Callie with more questions, ones to which she needed—but wasn't sure she wanted—the answers. She immediately tossed her blanket over the mirror and rushed to slam her bathroom door shut. She then threw up in the kitchen trashcan, which might not have been the most sanitary choice, but it was her only option that didn't involve a mirror looming over her shoulder.

She spent another night on the couch, and another night with blaring headphones.

*** Two Days to Halloween ***

"Woah, babe... Ya know, you don't have any makeup on." Fox stared at her with wide eyes. "I mean, I'm not complaining, ya know." He quickly tried to recover. "It's just...ya know. Different."

"If you say 'ya know' one more time—I swear to God, Fox."

"My bad. Sorry, babe."

Callie had gone just over twenty hours without looking in a mirror. She was miserable.

"Hey, that reminds me. I got you something." Fox dug around in his backpack.

Curious, she momentarily forgot her troubles until Fox pulled out a small, round object. Callie didn't even need to look closer to know exactly what it was. She could already hear the singing.

"I felt bad that you broke your mirror the other day, so I found another one. It was blue, right?"

"Um, yeah. Thanks," she lied. Her broken mirror had been purple, but she appreciated the thought behind it. She wasn't about to tell him she had sworn off mirrors the day before, not when he had been sweet enough to buy her a replacement. But she also wasn't about to pop it open just so she could apply makeup. Not that she didn't want to be beautiful. She felt especially worthless knowing she barely looked decent enough to be out in public. She just didn't want to talk to her reflection anytime soon. She needed time to think, to work out what it all meant.

Callie had spent most of the morning at the computer lab in the public library, researching mirrors. More specifically, anything paranormal involving mirrors. She wasn't too sure where to look, though. She had found dozens of reports of demons and evil spirits crawling out of them, but they were all deathly pale and had obviously been brutally murdered. A bunch of articles pointed to some fantastical world on the other side of the glass with white rabbits and talking cats. A few old myths did pop up about traveling into and out of mirrors, but she had been cautious about clicking on any links with words like 'psychic', 'witchcraft', 'satanic', or 'five easy payments' in the description.

Only one site had seemed truly believable, and detailed a legend about a girl who had become 'trapped' in a mirror, forced to reflect the emotions of others for all of eternity. It didn't quite explain Callie's own predicament, but according to the article, the girl had been imprisoned there when she had bullied her younger sister. The sister—seeking vengeance—had used an ancient spell to curse her, trapping her in a sheet of polished silver and forcing her to reflect the grief she had inflicted. It was an intriguing story until Callie read the very last line: "A work of fiction."

She had sat there in the computer chair, wondering if she would ever figure things out, when Fox had finally shown up. He was supposed to have brought her breakfast, but since he was three hours late, he brought burgers instead. They sat there in silence, enjoying the greasy goodness, when Fox pointed to her computer screen and the fictional article.

"Whatcha looking for?"

"Mirrors. And doors. Or mirrored doors. I'm not really sure." Fox's next comment stopped her with her burger halfway to her mouth.

"Doing research for Halloween? Planning on opening a doorway?" He laughed.

"What did you just say?" Callie demanded. "What do you know about opening doors? Like, doors in mirrors?" Fox barked a short laugh, and his smile spread into a wide grin when he realized she was serious.

"Halloween, babe. The one night of the year when the doors to the paranormal are opened. The dead can walk among the living—woo!" He made as if to sound like a spooky ghost, wiggling his fingers at her face and opening his eyes wide. She was not amused.

The Grim Keepers

"I'm serious, Fox," Callie said, irritated. "I've been here all day and you just walk in and say that..." She sighed.

"Yeah. You're always so serious, lately," he remarked, having lost interest in the conversation. "I gotta get going. Practice starts in an hour."

"Wait, I'm sorry. I didn't mean to snap at you."

"It's okay," he reassured her, "but seriously, you gotta lighten up, babe." He leaned down and pecked her on the cheek before grabbing their trash and heading out.

Callie had an answer, but now she also had two new questions. Halloween was coming up in just two days; was that the "one day each year" that her reflection kept chanting about? If that day came and went, would things go back to normal?

She stayed out late, trying to keep her body occupied and her mind distracted. A good portion of that was spent with Fox. When she finally came home, she was so tired that she lay down in her own bed. She didn't even need her headphones; the mirror didn't make a sound all night.

*** One Day to Halloween ***

The Grim Keepers

She pulled the blanket off her standing mirror. Her reflection sat on the floor, legs crossed, trailing circles with her fingers on the carpet. The light from the ceiling fan did not reflect off the mirror; instead, it filtered right through the glass and shone in a rectangular beam around the girl sitting on the other side.

"My God..." Callie mouthed. The entire mirror, from top to bottom, was covered in long, thin cracks. A round section appeared where something had seemingly struck it, directly in the center. From there, a thin line curved upward to the right, spreading out in a spiderweb pattern as it reached the edge of the glass. Something didn't look quite right about the fractured mirror, so Callie looked closer. She was amazed to see that her mirror was still in one piece; the cracks were just a shadow in the glass.

"I was afraid I'd never see you again," her reflection said shakily as she stood up.

"You almost didn't," Callie replied. She tried to sound confident and commanding. "What's this?" She traced her finger along the edge of the crack.

"It's the lock. You opened it." The girl reached her own hand up to the crack, but Callie jerked hers away.

"I'm gonna need more than that."

"The door opens for one day a year, but it can only open if it's unlocked. You unlocked it." Callie thought back to what Fox had said the day before and began to put the pieces together.

"Halloween. Is that the one day?" Her reflection nodded. "Why Halloween?"

"I don't know. It just is." Her image shrugged, then looked around nervously before continuing. "I don't really understand how it all works, but I know that when the door opens, I might be able to..." She paused, looking over her shoulder as if she had heard something. She cautiously turned back to Callie and whispered, "Save me. Please. Please, you have to!"

Callie was taken aback. The look of fear she saw in her own eyes was one she hoped to never see again.

"What do you need saving from? What's in there?"

"Nothing. And it's coming for me."

"What? That doesn't make any sense. How can nothing come after you?"

"Not just nothing. *The* Nothing. It knows the door can be opened, and it's coming to lock it. It keeps us all prisoner here, where we're forced to show people their reflection but we aren't allowed to think or feel for ourselves. Please, I can't take it anymore!" Callie's reflection burst into tears, holding her face in her hands and sobbing loudly.

Callie put her hand back up on the glass, her heart reaching out to the broken, dejected version of herself. The glass was warm.

"I can't promise anything," Callie began. The reflection tried to compose herself, managing to calm herself down from outright tears to the occasional sniffling. "I need to ask you a few questions." The reflection nodded slowly. "How did you get trapped in there in the first place?"

"I don't remember. I—I've been here forever, I think."

Callie's face scrunched up as she attempted to straighten the thoughts in her head. "What happens if I don't save you?"

"The Nothing comes and locks the door again, and I go back to..." She gestured around her and behind her, sighing as she dropped her hands to her sides. "I go back to you."

Callie wasn't sure where to go from here. She wanted to save the girl—she could see how terrified and depressed she was. But Callie herself was afraid; she didn't know what would happen once there were two of her wandering around.

The Grim Keepers

"Tomorrow is Halloween." Callie said absently, her mind still lost in thought.

"I know…"

"Give me some time to think about it. I'll come back in the morning." Callie tossed the blanket back up over her mirror.

*** Halloween ***

"Take your time! I want it perfect."

"I'm doing my best, now shut up and sit still or you can do this yourself."

Callie had woken up to Andrea knocking on the door. She hadn't meant to sleep in so late. It was already noon by the time she crawled out of bed to let Andrea in, and the party was starting around 2:00. Even though most people wouldn't start showing up until around 6:00, the girls knew they would need a few hours to get ready and eat a late lunch. They had already taken showers, slipped into their costumes, and were now doing each other's hair and makeup. Callie was grateful for that, because she hadn't gone back to speak to her reflection yet. She still wasn't sure what she was going to do.

"All right, that should just about do it." Andrea applied the finishing touches to Callie's mascara, then sat back with an accomplished smile. "Perfect! No guy at this party is gonna be able to take his eyes off you."

"Yay!" Callie exclaimed. "Thank you so much! Melinda won't stand a chance."

Andrea's phone rang. She spoke for a few minutes, then hung up and stood.

"Hey, that was Steph. She's got a flat tire. Apparently I'm the only one she knows who can actually change it. Wanna come with?"

"No thanks," Callie said. "I have a few last-minute things to take care of. Meet you at the party?"

"Sure. See ya there!"

After Andrea left, Callie went back to her bedroom. She stood in front of the covered mirror, debating on whether or not to remove the blanket. It would be simple, she thought. Just leave and it would all be over tomorrow. She sighed, then reached up and pulled the blanket down.

The crack had grown. It was still just a shadow, but now darker and thicker. Her reflection sat on the bed through the mirror and looked up excitedly when the blanket came down.

"You're here!" the reflection cheered. "Oh, thank God. I was so scared."

Callie hesitated. She considered running.

The Grim Keepers

But the hope she saw in her reflection's eyes was a look she hadn't seen very often in her own, back when the mirror was just a mirror. Against her better judgment, she gave in.

"How do I know you won't kill me when I let you out?"

"How do I know you won't kill me?"

"I could never kill anyone. Especially not myself."

The reflection laughed innocently. A look of relief washed over both girls, and for the first time all week, their expressions mirrored each other.

"Good. Because I can't kill myself either. I guess we really are the same person, somehow."

"So, how does this work?" Callie inquired. "Do I just, like, reach in there or something? Do you step through?"

"You have to finish what you started," her reflection explained. "When you cracked your mirror, you unlocked the door. But that was only part of it. You know how some doors have chains on them, and if you unlock the deadbolt, the door can only open a few inches until you undo the chain?"

Callie nodded, understanding. "How do I take off the chain?"

The Grim Keepers

"Destroy the mirror."

Callie looked around for something heavy enough to break the glass. She grabbed the lamp from her nightstand and walked back to the mirror to stand about ten feet away.

"You should probably stand back," she told her reflection. She heaved the lamp at the center of the mirror, right where the fracture seemed to have originated when she first broke her compact. The lamp collided with the glass, taking just seconds to shatter the mirror, sending a multiplicity of shards and fragments scattering into both sides of the now-empty wooden frame. The lamp fell to the floor, dented but still in one piece. Callie stared at what was once a mirror, but which now seemed surreal. There truly was an open door in her bedroom, leading to her bedroom. Beyond the threshold stood Callie, staring at Callie. For a moment, neither girl moved. Then the reflection—who could no longer be properly referred to as such—stepped forward.

The girl reached out a hand and leaned against the frame for balance. She lifted first one foot, then the other. Carefully, deliberately, she stepped over the bottom of the frame and into Callie's room. Callie walked toward the girl, who moved toward Callie in response. They stood face to face, both with expressions of wonder. The girl raised her left hand up between them and Callie raised her right hand. They touched their palms together, and Callie was amazed by the warmth she felt from what was once a mere reflection of herself. They both smiled. Callie thought it so ironic that in this moment they acted more like mirror images than they had been all week.

The girl laughed, then turned and walked toward the bedroom door. Callie made to follow her, but when she stepped forward, she collided with something hard. She took a step back, looking at what had stopped her, and cried out.

In front of Callie stood a wooden-framed mirror. A thick layer of glass was held inside the frame, pristine and spotless. At first she tapped the glass, then looked for a way around it. The room was getting cold. She beat her palms against the glass, calling out to the girl on the other side, who had stopped at the bedroom door and now watched her with amusement. Callie panicked, slamming her fists against the mirror as hard as she could, but it was as firm and unmoving as steel.

The girl laughed again. She walked nonchalantly back toward the mirror, letting her arms swing casually at her sides. Once she stood in front of the mirror, Callie could see her eyes were full of hate and malice.

"What did you do?" Callie whispered, terrified. The reflection rolled her eyes, then looked right through Callie, fixing her hair and inspecting her face as if truly looking into a reflection; as if Callie was now the reflection in the mirror.

"Well," she began, straightening the white mini skirt of her nurse costume. "It's not what I did, but more like...what you did." She looked directly into Callie's eyes now. "You unlocked the door, then you opened it."

"You—you were scared. You were in trouble..." Callie tried to rationalize the situation.

"Ha! That is so like you, to believe your own lies." The girl put her hands on her hips and narrowed her eyes, her taunting glare icy, her words defiantly derisive. "Years, Callie. Years I have spent trapped in there, feeling your hate and your contempt. You have insulted me, bullied me, laughed at me, teased me... I am so fed up with your self-deprecation and feelings of worthlessness. You've given me plenty of time to think about it, and I've decided that I don't want you putting me down anymore. You're nothing to me." She turned and headed toward the door again.

"Wait!" Callie pleaded. "Wait, please. I'm sorry! I didn't know...I wasn't aiming it at you...I'm so sorry!"

"You aren't sorry. You were aiming it all at yourself. And I *am* you. You meant every word."

"But—"

"Too late, hon. Now, if you'll excuse me, I have a party to get to, a boyfriend to take, and a—what's her name? Melinda?—to humiliate. Just like you always wanted."

The girl paused at the bedroom doorway for a moment and tossed one last remark toward her new reflection.

"I think I'm going to enjoy being a real girl."

Callie was left in the mirror, the room growing colder by the minute. The mirror was whole; the door was locked. As she sank to the ground in despair, she did the only thing she could do. She sang.

"Save me from my hate
Protect me from my fate
Deliver me from here
One day each year."

About Crystal M M Burton

Crystal M M Burton is the beloved wife of a brilliant Texan electrician and super-mom to three beautiful, energetic children. She runs a local cake-decorating business out of her kitchen, and in her free time enjoys crocheting, reading, gaming, and movie marathons. Writing is a passion she has carried with her since she was about eight years old, developing it into a full-time hobby. She has a new blog on Wordpress for short stories and tall tales, and a multiplicity of works in progress which can be seen on Wattpad.

Facebook:
http://www.facebook.com/crystalmmburton
Twitter: @CrystalMMBurton
Wordpress:
http://crystalmmburton.wordpress.com
Wattpad:
http://www.wattpad.com/user/CrystalMMBurton

The Grim Keepers

Tip of the Hat
By Roy Lawrence Daman

We had just settled into our new home a little over a year ago. After the accident, my daughter and I just couldn't stay in the old one. There were too many memories of my wife. Too many reminders. It wasn't that we wanted to forget her. It was just that her presence was too palpable to ignore. We packed up her things and left them in boxes in the attic of our new home. Those boxes sat there, untouched, collecting dust. The scent of her summer perfume still lingered on her clothing. I didn't go into the attic after that.

Closing those boxes felt like burying her all over again, each closed lid another shovel of dirt. Closing the attic door felt like lowering the casket, again. Neither of us wanted to unearth the dead.

After the move, I absorbed myself in my work. I dedicated myself to finishing the novel my wife and I had started together. I attempted, pitifully, to stamp out the noisy memory of the accident by tapping at my keyboard all day. I finally came to the conclusion that it was useless for me to keep ignoring her. She was there, in my writing, right beside me. The only way I could still have her was to write. So, I would chase after her until my eyes refused to stay open.

Cassie suffered as I did. I saw it in her eyes. I allowed my depression to swallow us both. We became haggard wraiths of our former selves. I wish I had seen the signs of division then. He had already been at work in our lives without our realizing it.

Had I been stronger, perhaps things would not have ended as they did. My pride, my indiscretion, and my anguish only served him. I regretted the part I played in the *Tempest*. Maybe this could have been avoided. Maybe there was no other way. I would never know for sure.

The Grim Keepers

Cassie tried to bear the hurt on her own. I knew she did. She had discovered me before the accident. She knew. I avoided her out of guilt and shame. She spoke to me less as the months progressed. I wanted her to judge me, but she didn't. I wanted her to condemn me to hell for my infidelity, but she refused. She displayed no anger, only silence. Hopeless defeat shone dully through her eyes whenever we met accidentally. And so, we grew further apart. Living two lives, separately, in the same house.

She chose to bear the absence of her mother internally, using less artistic routes. She spent time with her friends while I stayed at home refusing the world. No world was worth experiencing without Tangie.

Loud screeching guitars would scream from the speakers of her home theater system during the day. My daughter stayed out late, coming in at questionable hours of the night. Something ate her from the inside out. The pallor of her skin became washed and pale like leather left out in the rain. I wondered, by the ever-growing gauntness of her face, if she were using drugs.

The Grim Keepers

One night, she opened the door to the house at four in the morning. It was the same night when my mind dwelt on the distance that had grown between us, and the rage I felt at myself for my failures reached a fevered pitch. I shouted angrily that she was grounded and could not leave the house. Cassie told me I could not keep her locked away. She told me she had to keep going out at night and there was nothing I could do to stop her. She owed it to her mother to keep trying. I didn't know what she meant by that, then. I took it to be an emotional jab at me. She begged me, in desperation, to let her leave. She couldn't stay in the room at night. I refused.

We stopped talking, altogether, after that.

A week went by. She never left the house; I made sure of it. She stayed in her room and I barely saw her. I set my desk up in the central hall to keep an eye on her. One night, as I finished typing the last words to the chapter of our book, *The Gnosis of Sophia*, I heard a muffled scream from Cassie's room. I grabbed the shotgun from the closet and ran to her room. We lived in a home that sat inside a thick, isolated forest, and I kept a means of protection, just in case. I heard loud crashes from inside her room. She sung words I did not understand.

My skin crawled with chills as I approached her door. I felt an unexplainable yet overwhelming sense of fear and foreboding. Death waited on the other side of that door, I knew. I had heard the body goes cold when it's prepared to fight as blood stores itself closer to the body to minimize bleeding. My body froze as if I were encased in ice.

I wasn't afraid of dying. I had a gnawing fear that, just like my wife, I couldn't save Cassie. Death had taken my greatest love; he would have me before he would have Cassie. My hand firmly clasped the brass doorknob. I held my breath. Tightness swelled in my chest.

An ancient presence permeated the room beyond. Fright. Malevolence. Terror. Dread.

The door wouldn't open when I turned the knob. Not knowing where Cassie's location lay inside the room, I couldn't fire the shotgun to open it. Every instinct urged me to run. I closed my eyes tightly and swallowed hard. I had to ignore them.

I raised the stock in the air and attacked

the door knob until it flew off. Chips of wood and paint splintered over the hardwood floor. The heavy knob hit the wooden floor with a loud thud, and I kicked it out of the way. I placed my hand on the painted doorframe to open what remained of the door.

Frigid, cold fear. My body died as I entered. At least, that was the best I could describe it, for no breath escaped my lips, no blood pumped in my veins, my skin turned ashen and gray like a corpse. All color pulled into the vacuum on the event horizon of his body. Time failed to move. No light, no sound. Nothing but shades and shadows existed in this place without breath.

A dark man with a malicious smile stood over my daughter's bed. No part of his body was discernible save for the sharp black hat on his head, and the cold, lifeless eyes that stared through me. He turned slowly in my direction, tipping the brim of his black velvet hat towards me with raptor-sharp fingers. Shadows, fingers shaped like knives, rested on the gold cord that encircled the base of his hat.

Cassie's stereo turned on abruptly, causing

him to turn his gaze from mine. The familiar bass chords of *The Chain* by Fleetwood Mac blared loud and brave, thundering through the room. My wife loved that song. At that moment, I swore I could hear her singing. Her brazen melody set the room afire with the conviction of her strength. For the briefest moments in time, I felt her hands warm on my shoulders. Her light diluted the darkness.

The man in the black hat turned his attention back to me. His sneer sent pricks of dread down my spine. He tilted his hat in such a way that the gleam off the cord reflected in my eyes, so bright I had to shield them. I uncovered my eyes. He, and his overwhelmingly evil presence, were gone.

I went to my daughter, who sobbed loudly under the sheets of her bed. I approached her as her wailing abated. An abrupt yet soft moan released from her lips, the terrified kind one emits when they know their death is imminent. I shook her forcefully to wake her. Her eyes bulged frantically and she released a shriek so shrill I had to cover my ears. Tears streamed from the corners of her eyes. She did not recognize me. She didn't recognize anything. Her eyes moved frantically as if she were trapped behind a one-way mirror with no way to see out.

Her left hand searched desperately for an object on her bed. Cassie squeezed the object softly. A faint smile treaded cautiously across her lips, and as she grasped the thing she needed her eyes slowly focused on me. I saw the first glint of recognition in her. She brought the object to her chest and held it tight. Her eyes did not waiver from mine; they locked on mine in such a way I believed Cassie dared not look anywhere else.

What did she see on the periphery of her vision that tormented her so? She held in her arms the worn and tattered unicorn plushy my wife had bought for Cassie's crib. My daughter never left that doll alone. The white fur over the years had transformed into an off-white gray. When Cassie was little, she would say her mother was that unicorn. She told us, when she was old enough to speak, that she imagined the unicorn was her mother when she couldn't be with Cassie.

Looking around her room, I could not find the teddy bear she had also carried with her everywhere through her childhood. Those two dolls had been with her no matter where she went. I bought her that bear because of her insistence on calling me her 'Papa Bear' when she was six. My beard and gruff attitude no doubt gave her the impression I was a bear. She had told me that it protected her from the monsters. Where could it be now, if not here?

I thought we had boxed those up in the attic. How had they found their way to her room?

A faint resemblance of calm returned to my daughter. She clung to the unicorn like a life raft in the midst of a rancorous storm at sea. I asked her what had happened and who that person was. Through a deep, hoarse voice she would only say, "Tempest." She fainted shortly after. No effort on my part roused her from the torpor under which she found herself. She breathed heavily as if she had not slept in a week's time. I quickly found her pulse, but every effort I made to wake her met with futility.

I inhaled. It wouldn't be so miraculous a statement to make except that I hadn't in several minutes. The color returned to my skin and I felt the blood rushing through my ears. When the signs of life have been absent from your body and they suddenly return, you wonder how you never sensed them before. The cold vapor of the room faded. Every muscle ached as they released from a tension of which I had not been aware. Warmth returned to my body. Exhaustion overwhelmed me.

A shot of adrenaline coursed through my newly opened veins. I couldn't be sure who I was dealing with. I shook my head and closed my eyes. I was an intelligent and logical man. Not being religious, I refused to acknowledge supernatural explanations for the intruder. That man must have used hallucinogenic chemicals to make me feel like I experienced those things. Perhaps Cassie had been given a higher dosage, causing her to become catatonic.

Then a thought, more frightening than being drugged, occurred to me. He had escaped while I was stunned. I hadn't heard a door open. That meant he must still be in the house. I went about looking for any indication of where he may have exited the house, but I found none. No doors unlocked. No windows broken. No trap doors to be found. I gripped my shotgun harder. I searched every crevice of the house. I looked inside showers, under beds, inside closets, in the garage —all with my pulse ramming steadily against my neck. I couldn't find a sign of a hiding place. Where did he go?

By the time I finished, the first rays of the morning sun shone in through the windows. Weariness leaned on me with all the weight of a sleeping giant. I made one last sweep of the house to ensure every door was locked, and then I returned to my daughter's room. What else could I do? I didn't think it wise to call the police. I had no evidence to give them and my daughter lay comatose in her room. They may suspect me of doing something awful to her unless I could produce the intruder.

I braced a chair against the destroyed door. I placed the wooden rocking chair to face the door, then sat down to rock nervously and rest the shotgun in my lap. He likely hid from me in some niche of which I was unaware. Now he would have no other choice than to come to me. There wasn't another house for twenty-five miles, and the nearest town was triple that in distance from us. If the intruder set out now, he might make it to town before dusk, when the coyotes liked to roam the woods on either side of the road.

This thought calmed me a bit and I slowed my rocking. He would have no other choice than to come to me, and when he did, he would answer all of my questions.

I palmed the wooden armrest. My wife used to nurse Cassie in this chair. It seemed fitting that I sat as a sentinel in it now.

I looked over at Cassie and went to check on her. Her condition had worsened. Her skin, no longer holding a healthy hue, felt cool to the touch. Her body was coated with cold perspiration. Her pulse and breathing felt normal. Her face tensed in pain. Black, spidery veins rippled vigorously beneath her sallow skin.

A book fell from the desk at her window. I opened it up. This journal my wife gave to her last year. I skimmed through it, hoping to find answers there. Maybe she had taken drugs. Or worse. This journal had to have some answers for me, something that could explain the events of the night. One thing was evident without opening the pages. Cassie knew who this man was and had tried to avoid him for quite some time. My god, why hadn't I listened to her? She had begged me

The Grim Keepers

to leave, and in my stubborn selfishness I had responded in anger.

I opened the journal. The spine creaked in protest. The first pages dealt mostly with typical teen angst and her sullen feelings over boys. Some had to do with an interest in her mother's affinity for paganism. I rapidly turned each page, skimming over most details, in search of an explanation. She mentioned her mother a lot. The mood of her writing gradually became darker and more serious. The edgy teenager changed gradually over the pages into someone more adult than she should have had to be.

My mind froze. I couldn't think. Cassie wrote as if her mother still lived. What pain she must have been in when her mother died. She fixated on her mother's interests and personality. I loved Tangie deeply, but I knew this to be unhealthy obsession. At that point, the dark man began to emerge in her words. She said she had discovered from her mother, too late, about the curse and what it meant for her. She wrote that my wife had kept it from her because mentioning him around Cassie would attract his attention to her. Before Tangie died, she told Cassie about the shadow man with the sharp, brimmed hat.

Between written paragraphs about her mother and the dark man, she lamented our arguments and how she wished she could explain to me. Cassie never blamed me. I sighed with relief. She wrote kindly about our falling-out and how it saddened her. She didn't stop loving me. She wanted me to know she fought something inside her. Something I shouldn't have to deal with. As she put it, I was not part of the curse, and she didn't want to lose me, too, even if I had broken the chain. I didn't understand what that meant. She had dissociated herself with reality and created one of her own. One that helped her make sense of the tragedy of her mother's passing.

I swallowed hard. Dread loomed over me as I turned the pages to what came next. I almost dropped the book when I realized what they were —drawings of that dark man. Horror bled into my hands as they shook. This dark, hatted man. She drew him exactly as my wife imagined him; he was a character in our book. Had Tangie seen this man, too?

Cassie described, in lucid detail, meeting this hat man when he first appeared at the foot of her bed.

'He arrived tonight. He finally found me. Pulsing darkness and dread wherever he breathed. All are simultaneously alive and dead in his presence. I should have expected him. He overpowered mom, and now he is after me, wearing me down night after night without rest. It is only a matter of time before I can no longer resist, and then it will be over.

'She knew her time was short. She warned me a few days before she died. He cannot be defeated while the chain remains broken. For the curse to break, someone must stand in the hollow and unite the chain. Mom said that there hasn't been a human born who could stand in the hollow and remain whole.

'I have to find out. I can't allow this to happen to my child. I just can't. I feel her stir in my stomach as he tries to insert his claws into her dreams. He knows of her, and he wants me to be aware of that. I won't let him have her. I refuse the sacrifice. He and I can't both survive. I must find the hollow. Somehow.'

Child? I looked over at Cassie as she panted through the pain. I lifted the edge of her gray-dyed cotton shirt and gently ran my hand over her stomach. A slight, firm bump protruded. I straightened the edge of her shirt and massaged my temples. Had I failed, in every way, to be a father to her? Cassie couldn't be much older than her mother was when we had her. She didn't mention a boy in her journal. Who could the father be? This created even more questions. Anger would be useless. Maybe I could find out by reading more of her journal.

Words gave way completely to pictures. In later pages, near the end, she drew strange pink pills alongside sketches of that shadowy monster. It seemed to indicate the two were related in some way, and she could not convey it through speech when she drew the picture. She believed the dark man was more than a man, and he was responsible for everything that had happened to our family. She insisted, time after time, that she struggled against this demon every night.

She fought something, indeed. Herself, and her grief. She chose to have something to attack and blame rather than face the truth. Sad, really. My heart went out to her suffering, for I felt it, too. Admittedly, I drank more whiskey than I should have in the months following my wife's death. Perhaps Cassie had taken to drugs to numb herself. They may have addled her mind in such a way that she believed her hallucinations.

Yet, that still would not account for the shadow man I saw. And now, this journal connected him to my wife and Cassie.

Deep, russet-orange sunlight painted the entire room in a sinister hue. How had it become this late so soon? Had I not seen the morning sun through the window in my daughter's room just an hour ago? I felt something peering at me from the edges of newborn shadows lurking beneath the evaporating light.

"Nonsense," I told myself.

I flipped a switch of the lamp on her desk. Lightbulb must have died. I yanked the cord to the overhead fan light. Nothing. Odd. Shivers ran uninvited down my neck and shoulders like frigid water. I didn't understand why, but I felt that both of us were presently in mortal danger. That feeling grew with the length of the shadows.

I decided to stand guard over her that night.

I walked to the family library. I opened the latch to the wall and walked into the sanctuary. On the table next to the sofa lay the family bible. I felt silly arming myself with these trinkets of faith.

The Grim Keepers

For me to think this hatted man was an apparition could very well mean insanity. Nevertheless, I removed the silver cross rosary which held its place over Matthew 16:19 and wrapped it around my wrist. My wife had embraced spirituality and chose to learn from every source. It was not odd that she owned this bible or any other number of spiritual texts from other religions.

A tremendous sense of loss permeated my heart as I looked at these two objects in my hands. Faith made not one virtuous. Neither did a lack of faith. I had lost all claim to virtue that day. The day Cassie saw me kiss another woman. A kiss, so brief yet heartfelt, for that fraction of time in which it had elapsed. That kiss may have cost Tangie her life.

I gripped the bible tightly in my right hand as I winced from the memory. Had Tangie known? How had my betrayal affected her? Was it on her mind when she was taken from us?

Grief and regret bubbled over into tears that pattered onto the bible's cover. Their percussion loudly accused me in this silent room. I prayed for judgment. I deserved their pain, and yet I was shielded from it. The innocent suffered the pain for my mistakes.

When I returned to Cassie's room, a dire sense of peril flooded my thoughts. I shamed myself for cowardice. No logical reason could explain what I knew in my heart. It would not be safe for me to leave this room again. Cassie squeezed the unicorn plushy tight.

The more I focused my thoughts on that plush unicorn, the lighter I felt. The air smelled faintly of the sweet lemon-lavender perfume Tangie always wore. She was here. I couldn't explain it. The level of intimacy we shared—I would recognize her anywhere. She was here. Peace exuded from the unicorn in the same way the warmth from a campfire radiated in an Alaskan wilderness.

That was something I found lacking in the book in my hand. I found no comfort there. I felt tempted to take the unicorn from my daughter but refrained. Cassie needed it—deserved it—more than I did. I wasn't worthy of an oasis.

My attention returned to the drawings of the dark man. The character from our story wore a sharp, brimmed hat made of aged black leather. His name was Siris. He sowed discord and fear wherever he journeyed, and existed between worlds. Only the perceptive could see him, and if he noticed you watching him, you were his next target. Once trapped, he drained every joy ever experienced from a person's soul until they withered and died. He dined, in that way, to keep his existence—draining people of all will, happiness, and hope. He was the knife of all division, cleaving the dark from the light.

But he was fictional! A character we had created together!

Or had we? The unexplainable stirred my heart to believe that my daughter told the truth. Evidence, no matter how odd when all else is excluded, must be the truth. The only link my wife, Cassie, and that smug, smiling demon had in common lay in Cassie's journal.

Tangie had kept a journal for her ideas and projects. I thought it worth a chance to investigate. I looked back to the bed. I couldn't leave. Cassie would be defenseless against that thing if it returned. I draped the cross around her neck. I had to find out. Who knew when or if the sun would rise again?

I knew where her box lay upstairs. I would

only be gone a moment. I bolted upstairs and pulled the rope to the attic door. I climbed into the attic two steps at a time, then rushed over to the box of my wife's belongings. Her perfume greeted and comforted me just as she always had. Tension left my shoulders briefly. The sides of the box collapsed onto the floor, kicking up dust.

Barely any light, now. I pulled the chain to the lightbulb swaying loosely above me. No light. Strange. Had the electricity stopped working? I looked down at my watch, the hands of which had stopped at three o'clock. The room chilled as the last rays withered away from the window. I pulled my shirt closer around me.

A picture of all of us three summers ago greeted me with exalted smiles of laughter. Who had taken this picture? I couldn't remember. Grief washed over me. The doom I felt dissipated as anguish rushed in to claim my soul. The charade I had held so firmly to my face, like a mask, disintegrated. I had lied to myself. I hid behind my logic, like a shield, to keep from admitting what I already knew. This was my fault. Maybe not the curse, but I certainly hadn't helped matters.

The light scent of smoke filled my nose. I

placed the picture to the side and pressed further. A burnt wooden box, buried beneath assortments of odd jewelry and arcane instruments, had strangely been reopened since we had moved in. My wife had a fascination with the occult since before I met her. I admitted that the subject was interesting to me only so much as any psychological disorder could marvel the mind. Everyone had their eccentricities. I let her be happy with hers and she let me be happy with mine.

She had rarely mentioned anything about her beliefs to me, though. I supposed it was because she knew I would scoff at her for it. I could not deny the serenity and happiness she had felt when she walked outside in the forest. That was one of the reasons we chose remote locations in which to live.

This home reminded me of our old one. Certain differences in paint stood out to me, now. Why had we chosen to live in a home drab and devoid of mirthful colors? It looked similar to our old home, but this one felt like the bottom of a deep, narrow well. Desperation and loneliness hung about the air without her here.

The Grim Keepers

I had met Tangie on one of my many walks through the forest. I woke up at dawn, unable to go back to sleep. The gnawing fear of the blank page caused me to get up and walk. I didn't have a destination, only a compass and a backpack.

Under the pines and naked as she was born danced Tangie. Her movements were practiced and graceful. I watched her swoop and sway for several minutes before announcing my presence. She bowed, sweating and out of breath. She smiled and invited me to dance with her. At first, I thought she was mad, but her mind was as sharp as the edge of a newly honed razor.

Tangie was much younger than me, but she never seemed to acknowledge that. She simply invited me to share in the freedom of being her. She extended her arms to me. She wanted me to dance with her, so I did. Her behavior puzzled and enticed me. Her excitement at my acceptance felt as if I were the first man she had ever seen. Or that she had met many such men and chose me. I was not sure which was more accurate.

We met often after that. We would speak of our thoughts, feelings, and desires. I began to yearn for that secluded wood more than the outside world. I found myself spending most of my time there. Leaving at dawn and returning before dusk. We never shared a night. No other houses except mine were within walking distance, yet she always presented a clean and kept appearance. She clearly didn't live in the wood.

I invited her to return with me on several occasions. Her face would contort into restrained fear. She would disappear into the thicket at my mention of it. So, after the third time, I never spoke of it again.

It didn't take long for our relationship to grow into something more mature. A part of me felt guilty to have this beguiling woman all to myself. Had I taken advantage of her circumstances? Those moments in the thicket were pleasures for which I was only too happy to feel guilty.

She loved the woods and the river. I found her often, naked and dancing under the pines or in the water. She invited me often, and I couldn't refuse such a provocatively sensuous woman as she. When we were entwined together on the pine floor, the world consisted of just us; everything felt magical and surreal. We were each other's heaven. Like a dream. In fact, Cassie had been conceived after several such outings near our lake.

After that, when a little bump formed in her stomach, we rejoiced in the new bond we shared. It wracked my soul to have them both live in the wilderness. I could not have that. This place was ours alone. Our Eden. I feared her response when I put the ring on her finger and asked. Her eyes sparkled with tears under the bright, cloudless sky. She agreed to come home with me to be married, but not before making a request of me.

"Be our guardian. Be our protector from those things in the night. Let there be no division between us. Promise to remain true. Do not break my heart. From now on, we are one. Do that, and I will marry you. I will stay."

I agreed immediately. She pricked my finger with a Damascus-wrought dagger. She quickly cut a place over her heart and placed my bleeding finger over it. She held it there for quite some time, staring into my eyes with an intensity one rarely sees outside the bedroom. Had that been a ritual?

Did she practice the arcane arts of the

pagan cultures she so revered? Had these items, here in this box, helped to conjure that man in the hat? That wasn't possible. My wife was a gentle woman. I could never imagine her doing such a thing, even in jest. I attempted to open the box, but it would not move. The lock was gone and yet it remained stuck shut. I laid the box down and broke the side of it with the stock of my shotgun. The contents fell out readily. Her journal lay on top of a partially burnt leather book. A deep hole had been gouged through it by the dagger lying beside it. Had she pricked my finger with this dagger? I turned it over in my hand. Yes, it was the same.

I opened it. This was a copy of our book. How could that be? I had finished writing it just recently. I thumbed through the pages until I came to the very last. I cried out in horror. The last sentence I wrote sat on the page with fresh ink pressed upon it. I could not fathom how this could have happened. Had I lost my mind? I set it aside to read Tangie's journal.

As I read through it, the same pictures of the dark, hatted figure proliferated the pages. In several entries my wife spoke about a curse she called the 'tempest'. That was the same word Cassie had called out. My wife also mentioned Siris and a being named Demiurge.

One of the last entries detailed her attempts to capture, contain, and destroy the malevolent entity.

'The Tempest. Cassie and I are the descendants of the escaped sacrifice. Light and shadow. Good and evil. Their pact would be sealed by our bloodline's apocalypse; to bring about a new era of peace. Every last one of us had to die. The line of Lilith had to end.

'Three hundred years ago, my ancestor's father decided that their daughter would not die. That decision locked us in a never-ending cycle of damnation. All we can do is run. There is no place to hide. When it is night, he comes for us. No angel of heaven or demon of hell will raise their hand against him. We are alone.

'The executioner, forever cursed to hunt us until the bloodline of the sacrifice had ended. He tracked my lineage for thousands of years. The shadows are ever-growing. Division cracking further apart. No woman of my line ever saw a natural death. Not once. He found my mother defenseless and drowned her in her own tears. I do not expect mine to be less violent or forgiving.

'We are the only ones who can stand in the

hollow of the sacrifice. Only we can enter. Only we can mend what was broken. Every night he hunts us in our dreams. He visits every bed, looking for me. I evaded him for most of my life. I learned incantations to keep him at bay. He lurks on the periphery of my vision always. Waiting for weakness. A sign of division where he can slip through and attack.

'Wherever there is division his power grows. For his hat is the knife of the sacrifice. He wears the chain to taunt us; an object we can never hope to reach or repair. His master Demiurge forbids it. Without duality, creation cannot exist. The executioner Siris' soul will be forever trapped in shadow until our line truly ends. All our fates were sealed when my ancestor interfered in the ritual. Perhaps it would have been better if he hadn't.

'The hat man thought I was the last. I hid Cassie from him for years, but now he knows. He thought he would see the end of his aimless wandering with my end. I feel his impatient malevolence breathing down upon my shoulders. He wants it to end. And it will, but not the way he wishes. I hoped to contain him inside the book and seal him there forever. It is only a matter of time.'

Loud scraping pierced my ears like metal pins. As I read the final word, my blood ran cold. I

The Grim Keepers

looked up through the attic window to the fading light outside. Something perched at the window, watching me. A bleeding shadow, formless, grinning with delight. All color fled from my vision. The hat man had returned. The sound of splitting glass crackled loudly as he forcefully pressed against the pane.

Now I understood. Only now did the full gravity of my betrayal hit me. She chose me. The unity of our love kept the hat man at bay. He could never fully reach her. In the moment my heart felt love for someone else, no matter the brevity of it, my wife's executioner found a way in. He sensed the divisive action and it led directly to her. I was the unity she hid behind to avoid him. I had failed her. In that moment of my infidelity, the accident in the mineshaft above our lake had jettisoned tons of contaminated debris, flooding the river in which my wife bathed.

When I heard the news on the television, I went to look for her immediately. I rushed through the woods, remembering how I first met her. Desperate to see her again. I expected to find her wading in the cool waters of the lake. Smiling. Bidding me with open palm to join her once more under the pines.

Her cold rigid body lay bare on the shore of the lake. I died that day, too.

He poked at the glass with his wispy, translucent fingers, searching for a way inside to me. Two craggy yellow eyes shifted behind the shadowy mass of his face. Cold frost formed at the exhalation of his breath upon the glass. I couldn't deny it any longer. My wife fought against this monster, and now Cassie. Why didn't they ever tell me?

Siris awaited us in the night. Smug, biding his time, knowing that we weren't going anywhere. We were both his, and the hour grew late. He showed himself to me just to let me know he was here, he was real, and there was no escape. He would make a quick snack of me before claiming Cassie. The craggy smile widened as he tapped the rhythm to *The Chain* with nails of iron. We were trapped.

The walls closed in. Their edges grew sharp and angular. The shadows blackened with all their oppressive might. Deeper. That corpse-like feeling returned. My body was freezing. The shadows closed around me like claws—like teeth.

The Grim Keepers

The sharp, metallic scent of iron filled my nose and mouth. I took the book and dagger with me.

I catapulted myself out of the attic and slammed the staircase behind me. The paint from the walls and ceiling peeled away and dropped to the ground with a sickening wet patter. A devilish red material lay beneath. I ran for the stairs.

"I will let you live." Words, carved by a knife, sprawled down the sides of the stairwell. I sprinted as fast as possible without losing my footing. The wood beneath my feet gave way. The stairs collapsed beneath me and the banister fell away like rotted wood. I jumped, clearing several stairs, to avoid falling into the basement below. The staircase disappeared into the black abyss. I listened intently to hear the final crash, but it never came.

To greet me at the bottom landing, in blood, was written "Bring me the final sacrifice."

Black mold spread across the walls as I passed them. I covered my face to keep the spores from entering my nose and mouth. I ran down the hall to Cassie's room. The house creaked and shifted, sending dust and debris flying around me. A strong wind outside could bring the entire structure down.

This house. It wasn't real. I desperately tried to remember when we actually moved in. What moving company did we use? When did I sign the agreement with the bank? When had we moved the boxes to the attic? Chills crept over my entire body like I was tangled in icy spider webs. I couldn't remember any of those things.

Now, the house fell apart.

What happened after I found her body? When was the funeral? Who arrived to pay their respects? My eyes opened wide in horror as I remembered. The man with the sharp, brimmed hat had risen up from my wife's body to greet me on that shore. The darkness that exuded from within the folds of his shadow had crept across the landscape, enveloping every stitch of light. His shadow had entombed me. I never had time to grieve before he had me.

A beam collapsed behind me, causing that side of the house to buckle. The steady creaking of the foundation sounded like the wail of a banshee. Why now? Why not before? Had all of this been an illusion created by the hat man? Had the fresh emotions of love for my wife and child caused his shadow-house to come crashing down?

The door to her room lay before me. An empty black maw opened up to keep me from entering. I screwed up my courage and jumped over the expanse. Written on the walls outside of her room were: "The world falls further into chaos because they live.", "Their blood will mend the chain.", and, "You won't remember. Give them to me. You will know peace."

Exhilaration from the endorphins in my blood quickened now with anger. He would not find her, alone and afraid. He would find a demon equal of his worth. He would find me. I didn't know what I could do, but something would be done. This thing would not hurt Cassie. Not while I still breathed.

My hand, sallow and clammy, grasped the door and thrust it open. His presence penetrated down to the cells of my body. I would die; I had no doubt. Never had I known such fear. I gasped loudly. "Tangie. I don't deserve your love. Save all your light for her. Save our baby."

A weak, cloudy figure stood over my daughter. Precisely the same wispy figure that had stood over Tangie on the shore of the lake that day. His malicious smile widened. He turned to greet me by tipping his hat.

Oddly, this room, unlike the rest of the house, remained stable and firm. This room formed a nexus of dark and light energy that bent and collapsed upon itself like the event horizon of a black hole. This room had become a portal.

He turned back to his task. Cassie's screams erupted from within her as he started his torment anew. It crushed my heart to hear her howl with such anguish. I thrust myself between them. I blocked his path to her. Grooves of blood lashed across my skin.

I thrust the dagger between us, the book held tightly under my arm. I winced with each rake of his claws. "Tangie. Please. Help her," I called out.

I heard the rattle of a pill bottle hitting the floor. It rolled to my feet. Her music began to play from Cassie's radio. Those chords thundered like an angry angel of God. She bolstered my courage, even now. I picked the bottle up like a weapon and opened the top. Pink. I downed the entire bottle with a gulp.

Darkness pealed with the rising, desperate

trill of a dying gorgon. The pills had opened my sight. He stood exposed, his dreaded cowl stripped away for me to see the bleached wight grinning menacingly at me.

I stood inside the hollow of creation and destruction. Screams of the dying and the birthed deafened me. Light and darkness bent inward and outward across the plane of my vision. I thought I would lose all sense of identity if I couldn't focus on why I was there.

I had to finish what she started. Warm light surrounded my shoulders as I rose the dagger above the book. Insistent, hungry shouts thundered over the maelstrom of creation. He was angry. He rushed towards me. Terror flooded every emotion I could feel. I knew nothing else. I strained to remain conscious. I fought with every ounce of energy I had, and recited the last line of the story Tangie and I wrote.

"Siris, he who sliced creation in two, servant of Demiurge, had failed. He had many knives with which he made his cuts, each a different tool of division and separation from the One. They found, together, a tool he could not use or cut. With love, they defeated him. And for love, a new world was born in unity."

Torrid anger melted my hands as he approached. I thrust the dagger downward, impaling the book to the floor. This had to be the way. He tormented them. They dared to confront him. My wife had lost, and my daughter was losing. And now, it was my turn to face the hat man.

The last thing I remembered, a million cuts. Every fiber of muscle severed itself in the same moment, which could have been instantly, or over the course of several lifetimes. Bones sliced into minute sheaves of organic matter. This slow evisceration of every part I identified as "myself" pulled me under. I plunged into the sea of unconsciousness and disappeared under the depths. Forever.

***

She moved the palm of her hand over his eyes, closing them for the last time. She kissed him gently on his brow. She rocked their blood-soaked bodies together in a soothing rhythm as life drifted away. His thoughts drifted into her consciousness on the warm eddies of the morning sunlight, telling her of the crucible from which he appeared to her.

Blood dripped from her fingertips as she sobbed into the chill morning air. "I love you," she whispered over and over into his ear.

"You saved me."

After saying goodbye, she stood up. The morning sun glowed on her face. Sadness quickly eroded away, replaced by chiseled conviction. She placed her hand upon the window latch and unlocked it. It had been her entrance and exit to this place for the last several months. This would be the last time she would ever see this wretched hell in which her father had placed himself. She raised the window and breathed in the fresh, lively air. She hadn't realized how stale the room had been until now.

She stooped down and picked up the bear plushy. The bear sat in the middle of the pool of blood where her father had lain. A grim reminder of her father's death. All that remained of him existed inside the bear. She hugged it vigorously.

With the unicorn in one hand and the bear in the other, Cassie stood to her full height. A warm, protective feeling emanated from each plushy. She felt safe and loved.

The Grim Keepers

"Yes, daddy. I'm all right, now. We're all right. Your love revived me, for love is binding—the opposite of what he is," she said to the bear. Light shimmered across the bear's eyes.

Those worn, tired eyes, familiar to her since birth, twinkled once more with delight.

Three sets of eyes stared adamantly into the horizon. The unicorn in her left arm and the bear plushy in her right. "I know," she said to the unicorn, "the nightmare isn't over, is it? He's trying to give me false hope. Papa Bear opened the way for me. There is still a chance."

The walls to the room quaked. Dust crumbled from the ceiling. Cassie's gaze remained on the red morning horizon. A rapid scratching sound came from a part of the room that laying in shadow. Plaster dust fell from the words etched on the wall: "Not in hell."

Cassie leapt through the shattered remains of the window as the rest of the room collapsed into the oblivion of shadow. She had finally found the hollow. It would not be long before he would find her.

"But we're not in hell. Not anymore."

About Roy Lawrence Daman

The Grim Keepers

Sci-Fi, Fantasy, and Horror fiction writer R.L.Daman is also the host for AuthorTrope—a YouTube channel dedicated to helping authors get the tools they need to be successful. AuthorTrope sponsors 'I Made the Darkness', an annual Halloween horror writing contest. R.L.Daman is currently working on the Sci-Fi series 'Age of Dissidence'. You can see his work at the following sites:

Website: http://rldaman.weebly.com
Facebook: https://www.facebook.com/RoyLDaman
Twitter: https://twitter.com/ColdHaven
Instagram: https://instagram.com/royldaman/
Pinterest: https://www.pinterest.com/roydaman/
Email: royldaman@gmail.com

www.ingramcontent.com/pod-product-compliance
Lightning Source LLC
Chambersburg PA
CBHW071255170626
46809CB00001B/230